ARTIE'S BARK

Best Wishes

Jason Jarvie

ARTIE'S BARK

JASON SAVIO

WFP
WORDFIRE PRESS

EBook ISBN: 978-1-68057-389-3
Trade Paperback ISBN: 978-1-68057-388-6
Dust Jacket Hardcover ISBN: 978-1-68057-390-9
Library of Congress Control Number: 2022946254

Cover design by MiblArt
Kevin J. Anderson, Art Director
Published by
WordFire Press, LLC
PO Box 1840
Monument CO 80132

Kevin J. Anderson & Rebecca Moesta, Publishers

WordFire Press eBook Edition 2022
WordFire Press Trade Paperback Edition 2022
WordFire Press Hardcover Edition 2022
Printed in the USA
Join our WordFire Press Readers Group for
sneak previews, updates, new projects, and giveaways.
Sign up at wordfirepress.com

for Oscar

"With a knick-knack paddywhack,
Give a dog a bone,
This old man came rolling home."

—Children's song

Be careful what you wish for.

—Old proverb

ONE

Evelynn Crofton wished she never woke up on that humid spring morning, but the sheets were sticking to her back and the sunlight sneaking in through the broken blinds was hurting her eyes. Mrs. Skittles needed to be fed, anyway.

That's what she called her long-haired cat, along with an assortment of other nicknames that most people would probably snicker at if they ever heard them. And the times that Mrs. Skittles was naughty and stuck her sharp little claws out were the times that Evelynn yelled naughty words at her in a fiery spat. She always asked for forgiveness later, amen.

Evelynn rolled her rotund self out of bed, letting the pink flowered sheets peel off her sweaty back, and reached over for her white nightgown on the chair nearby.

"Mrs. Skittles?"

Usually, the cat was snooping around somewhere in the bedroom when she woke up. Sometimes, though, the cat liked to sleep in the dirty laundry hamper and relieve herself in it. On this particular morning, with no Mrs. Skittles brushing her furry tail against her leg, Evelynn was leaning toward the latter.

"Goddamn cat," Evelynn said, getting herself up. "If you're

pissing on my drawers again, you'll spend the rest of the week outside."

Evelynn finished putting her flowing nightgown on in a huff, looking like a ghost that haunts its victims' fridges. Casper the Hungry Ghost.

She once was married to an accountant by the name of Walt. One day, Walt had enough of being told he was useless and playing second in favorites to Mrs. Skittles, so he decided to blow his brains out. *So be it,* Evelynn would often think to herself when she walked past Walt's favorite chair in the living room, an uncomfortable-looking thing fading from green to a musty yellow color. *If you don't want to be here with us then we don't want you here anyway.*

What Evelynn wanted right now was to find her cat and cook up some morning eggs with cheese.

"Where are you my little miracle?" she called out as she made her way into the kitchen.

No sign of any miracle, just a half-empty bowl of dry cat food and leftover pork chops from dinner she apparently forgot to put in the fridge the night before. She opened the fridge and put the dried-up, barbeque-drenched chops inside without any tin foil. Evelynn didn't mind that nice zesty flavor that only a fridge can add to your meal. Problem was, she could have sworn she put the leftovers away before she went to bed. She also would have sworn on her TV Guide collection that she had a full carton of eggs. Right now, all she saw was an empty case staring back at her, except for a lonesome-looking egg at the end of the top row.

She took the egg out and studied it. Some foreign substance, similar to the orange guts you pull out from inside a pumpkin when carving a jack-o-lantern, stretched across it. A warm heat radiating off of it startled her and she dropped the egg, cracking it on the floor. Bending down to pick it up, Evelynn saw another egg shell cracked and spread across the floor, and another, and another, all leading out of the kitchen. She followed the path of egg shells like an older and less graceful version of Gretel, all the way right up to the front door.

With the discovery of each egg shell, Evelynn became more and more furious. Yolk strained across the blue carpet near the coat rack.

"Mrs. Skittles?"

Evelynn, in all her nightgown glory, swung open the front door in a fit of rage, expecting to see her cat on its perch at the doorstep. Instead, what lay there was yet another egg shell. Four total now, and four too many if you asked someone who had planned on scrambled eggs for breakfast.

Pushing the screen door open, she followed the trail, leaving the door to close with a loud *CRACK!* behind her. She followed the mess of more egg shells and the strange orange substance that surrounded them all the way up to her mailbox.

Evelynn paused, looking around to see if any of her neighbors were watching. Mr. Sadly was apt to be home and peeking through his curtains at her. *The pervy old devil*, she thought to herself. Although the thought didn't really seem to bother her all that much.

"Mrs. Skittles! You goddamn pain in the ass," she said, immediately crossing herself in the name of the Holy Spirit. It was Sunday, after all.

The cat must have run off, but she'll be back later. And when she shows her prissy little self, I'll give her a good lesson.

A grin spread across Evelynn's face that would have made her late husband turn in his grave.

Not giving it a second thought, Evelynn opened her mailbox, hoping somewhere in the back of her mind that the weekly flyer would be in it with all the week's best deals at the local grocery store, especially another round of the buy-one-get-one free potato chips.

She stared into the black mailbox and froze.

The flyer was in there, sure enough. But something else was, too.

Slowly, she pulled the flyer out. *Buy one dozen eggs, get one free* it said in big, cheerful lettering. Evelynn paid no mind to the opportunity to fill her fridge with more eggs this week, although her intense gaze said otherwise.

"Mrs. Skittles?"

Atop the week's steals and deals, right next to the eggs on sale, Mrs. Skittles's small, lifeless head blankly looked back at Evelynn.

She screamed, sending Mr. Sadly running from his window.

TWO

The boys of Sunfish Lane always spent most of their springs and summers down the street at the ballpark.

None of them ever tried out for any of the school teams or signed up for an organized league. They just took it upon themselves to get together and have fun. Why should anyone be told whether or not they can play based on how good they are, or how much they can pay?

America's old pastime is meant to be enjoyed by everyone, no matter how fat your wallet is or how many times you strike out.

But there is no denying that it's always more enjoyable when you're hitting the ball and not swinging at thin air.

"Wow, you need glasses, Tommy?" Jerry Redman asked from the pitcher's mound, pushing his black-rimmed glasses back up to the top of his nose. His long, brown bangs stuck out from under his backward ballcap and disappeared behind the rims of his thick glasses.

Tommy Watson, with his own sweaty mop of hair poking out from his frontwards-facing ballcap, had swung through the second pitch Jerry delivered him. The two looked a lot like brothers, both with genuine smiles that also had a hint of mischievousness. The only difference was that Jerry usually followed through with what lay behind that grin, while Tommy knew better not to.

To Jerry's left stood the gangly, blond-haired Justin Dunn at first base, waving his hands up in the air in a "we give up" gesture. The heavier-set Eric Covitz, who was catching behind the plate, had seen this all before and knew how it would play out.

Jerry loved to razz his friend Tommy as he threw heater after heater.

"Just keep it coming, Jerry. Or are you afraid you can't get me out?" Tommy said back with that smile.

"Oh, I can get you out. I can get you out like Sarah Lackey's belly button."

"How do you know Sarah Lackey has an outie?" Justin asked, dumbfounded.

"Wait, what's an outie?" Eric asked from behind the plate.

"'Cause she showed me," Jerry said with his patented wry expression.

"Yeah, right! The only thing she's shown you is the back of her head in Mrs. Peterson's math class!"

Jerry ignored Justin's remark and kept his focus on Tommy. He blew a bubble from the gum he was chewing.

"Okay, Tom. Here it comes."

Tommy gripped the handle of the bat. The black rubber around the handle was old and peeling. Later, Tommy would have to wash his hands clean of what looked like a bunch of ants crawling on them.

Jerry leaned back and then heaved forward, throwing the ball with extra mustard at home plate.

Ding! The unmistakable sound of an aluminum bat and baseball making contact, piercing through the heat of a June day. The four friends watched the ball fly deep into right field. It landed with a flat and anticlimactic thud in the grass.

"And there he is," Eric said, standing up from his crouching position and pulling his catcher's mask up.

From around the corner, a short and chubby beagle appeared, running with all the excitement of a fan who just saw their team win the big one. The beagle made its way around the wooden logs used as fencing to separate the field from the road, and headed directly to the ball Tommy hit. The dog scooped the ball up in its mouth, stopped in its tracks, and looked up at its four spectators.

"There goes another one," Eric said, taking his glove off and putting his hand on his hip.

A smile escaped Tommy as he watched the beagle.

"Sorry, guys."

"Don't worry, Tommy. We're used to it," said Jerry, as he lifted up his ball cap to wipe sweat off his brow. "Same time tomorrow?"

"Yeah, if Tommy can get that ball back," Justin said. "You better start running now. Looks like he's got an extra kick in his step today."

The beagle pranced around with the ball in its mouth, egging them on before bolting back in the direction it came.

"He's got a head start on ya, Tommy!" Jerry yelled.

"Okay, see ya guys!"

Tommy ran over to the bench and grabbed his pack and continued on in the direction where the beagle had just been a moment before. The sun was breaking through the opening in the trees above, creating slices of sunlight along the same road Tommy had chased this beagle down time and time again.

He could see the dog trucking along about two houses down.

"Art, slow down!"

The beagle paused for a second, turned its head toward Tommy in acknowledgment, and then sped off again, going faster with all the energy of a puppy even though it wasn't one.

Tommy finally made it to the end of the street. Waiting for him at the corner, with the baseball placed neatly on the ground in front of him, was Artie, Tommy's dog and best friend.

"One of these days I'll catch up to you, Artie," Tommy said, bent over and panting with his hands on his knees. "Should've taken the bike today. I don't know what I was thinking."

Artie looked up at Tommy with his bright and loving eyes. Always looking for attention, Tommy gladly obliged him with a pat on the head.

"All right, let's go home and get you some lunch."

THREE

Nothing eventful ever happened on Sunfish Lane or anywhere in the town of Brighton Falls, for that matter. It was a quiet and peaceful coastal community in New England that got its kicks from small parades and sidewalk sales. So, when Tommy turned the corner onto his street with Artie by his side, he couldn't believe what he was seeing.

Ms. Crofton was in her front yard screaming and thrashing her arms around in her see-through nightgown. She could be a drama queen and everyone knew that, but the police officer parked in her driveway made Tommy think that maybe something else was going on other than the typical sideshow.

Artie must have thought the same, because he started barking at the two of them as he and Tommy walked by.

"Him!" Evelynn Crofton yelled, pointing at the beagle.

Evelynn propelled herself past the officer, right at Artie. Tommy had never seen her move so fast before. Suddenly, Tommy realized she wasn't going to stop. He picked Artie up and held him in his arms.

Evelynn reached out, trying to pull Artie away until Tommy had to push her back.

"Have you lost your mind?" Tommy said.

"He killed her! He killed her!" Evelynn cried.

She lunged forward at Artie again and the officer put his hands on her shoulders to restrain the heavy-set woman as best he could.

"Get your damn hands off me or I'll shout rape!"

"Ms. Crofton, I'm here to help you," the officer said.

Out of breath and panting as if she just ran a marathon, Evelynn Crofton finally stopped.

"Now why would you call this boy and his dog out?" the officer asked.

Evelynn gathered herself back up and held her head high in the air. Without looking at any of them, she said, "That damn dog is always running up and down this street every day. He thinks he has the run of the place."

She lowered her head back down to meet Artie's.

"But guess what?" she said, voice rising. "He doesn't! This is Mrs. Skittles's neighborhood and you can't take it from her!"

She ripped away from the officer and went at Artie again. Tommy jumped back.

"Go on, kid," the officer said. "Get out of here. I'm not keeping you here."

Tommy, a bit shaken, turned back for home without letting go of Artie, who gave Evelynn Crofton one final bark for the day before leaving her in a heap in her front yard.

"What the hell got into her?" Tommy asked Artie.

Artie looked at him quizzically, as if wondering the same thing.

FOUR

The school year was winding down for the students at Brighton Falls Middle School and there were only a few days left before the start of summer vacation.

When Tommy arrived at school the next day, he was surprised to see his friends still hanging around outside. Normally they'd run in to be the first to get the pancakes. The cafeteria food was notoriously gross. It was understood by everyone, however, that the pancakes were the exception.

"Hey, over here!" Tommy heard Justin say to him.

Justin and the others were huddled off to the side of the front entrance, having some sort of powwow and sharing the types of secrets only thirteen-year-old boys can come up with.

"What's going on?" Tommy asked as he approached them.

Eric turned toward him. "You didn't hear?"

Tommy shook his head.

"Oh boy, Tommarino, you're not gonna believe this," Jerry said with a crazed grin.

"Gross, just absolutely gnarly," Eric said. He had a look on his face that made Tommy think he was about to puke.

"Anyone going to tell me what's going on?" Tommy asked.

"That hot-air balloon Ms. Candy—"

"Ms. Crofton," Justin said, correcting Jerry.

"Ms. Crofton, Candy, whatever," Jerry continued, "her cat got torn to shreds."

"Not shreds, you idiot," Justin said. "Its head got torn off."

"What's the difference? It's toast either way."

"Are you guys serious?" Tommy asked. "She came after Artie yesterday, trying to blame him for something but she wasn't making any sense."

"Yeah, they found its head in the mailbox like someone left it there as a prank," Justin said. "That's what I heard Mrs. Langston saying to Mr. Welch when they walked in."

"How's that for a special delivery," Jerry said, with that same strangely amused smile spread across his freckled face.

"C'mon, Jeer, cut it out," Eric said.

"Did you see it, Tommy?" Jerry asked. "Did you see the head and the guts and the—"

"No, I didn't see anything. There was a police officer there. That was it."

"Who would do that to an animal?" Eric muttered. "I know that Crofton lady is obnoxious and nobody likes her, but why kill her cat?"

The group of friends paused for a moment, thinking it over, until Mr. Welch yelled at them from the top of the school entrance steps to get their lazy butts inside. They had missed breakfast and homeroom was already starting.

FIVE

It had been a dismal season for the Brighton Falls Bandits the previous summer, but Tommy and the gang had high hopes for the upcoming one. After finishing fifteen games below .500 and last in the eastern division, it could only go up from there for the Bandits. Artie was looking forward to it, too. At least, that's what Tommy liked to think. The two of them had never missed a game together, and Artie had become a type of team mascot for their hometown minor league ball club, something even Beebee the Bandit, the big-headed cowboy cartoon character getting paid to dance around in the stands, would have to admit.

"You ready, Art?" Tommy asked the excitable dog as he opened his desk drawer. The drawer was about as cluttered as the rest of Tommy's room, with comic books and toys thrown about the place. Above the desk in the corner of the room hung a poster of ballplayer Clint McCraw, an outfielder who used to play for the Bandits until he got called up to their major league counterpart, the Crusaders.

Tonight was the home-opener for the Bandits and Tommy was taking out Artie's Bandits bandana for him to wear (everyone had to have one—if you didn't then you weren't a true Bandolier, as they called themselves). Tommy sat down on the floor next to Artie and wrapped the bandana, with its Bandits cowboy logo patterned in between a red and blue outline, around the dog's small frame. He tied it carefully, making the perfect knot so it wouldn't fall off when Artie ran.

Artie looked down, inspecting his favorite old bandana—the same one he'd worn for the past twelve summers—and looked back up at Tommy. The beagle gave his friend a big lick on the face as if to say thanks.

"You're welcome," Tommy said with a laugh. "It still fits you like a tailored suit."

Tommy kissed Artie back on his right cheek, where his bones were beginning to show with his old age.

"Let's have a winning season, Art."

SIX

"Hey, you gonna finish that?"

"No, I guess not."

Tommy handed the rest of his popcorn over to Jerry, who already had himself a Bandits Burger (two patties with fried onion rings glazed in hickory smoke barbeque sauce) and a Shutout Shake (just vanilla ice cream and chocolate milk mixed together, but Jerry swore they put alcohol in it).

"Get ready for a long summer again," said Eric as he put his head in his hand.

Tommy and his friends had sat through seven innings of classic Bandits baseball: No runs for the good guys, plenty for the bad guys. With the lowly Providence Peacocks coming into town, the boys believed the Bandits had a chance to start the season off on the right foot.

They were wrong.

"It's just the first game. You never know," said Tommy.

"At least one of us is having a good time," Justin said, looking next to Tommy.

Artie, sitting by Tommy's side on the bleacher, saw something that caught his eye. He shot up out of his seat, barking and tail wagging.

It was his infamous adversary: The Bandits' official team mascot, Beebee.

"Art, you can stop," Tommy said. "He heard you."

Beebee gave the usual wave and continued on his way, taking pictures with the young boys and girls. The arms and legs of the person wearing the costume jettisoned out of the oversized torso like toothpicks, ending with big cartoon gloves and cowboy boots. Tommy wondered fleetingly how it was possible that none of the kids were scared to take a picture with such a bizarre-looking character. Tommy was never one to get his picture taken with Santa Claus or the Easter Bunny, no matter how hard his mother tried to make him. There was something about a person who hid behind a mask that made him feel uncomfortable. And, the older he got, Tommy was beginning to realize that not all masks are the visible type.

Artie didn't stop his barking, and some of the people sitting around him began to look.

"That's right, Artie. You tell him," Jerry said, chewing his popcorn. "I bet he can't even see them people he's taking pictures with!" He yelled this loud enough for Beebee to hear.

The top-heavy mascot, a nightmarish depiction of a cowboy, complete with a mustache and ten-gallon hat with a "B" adorned on the front of it, turned in the direction of Tommy and his friends, looking right at them with his dead, cartoon eyes. His big, fake smile and even bigger cowboy hat swayed from side to side as he walked through the stands.

Beebee, almost tripping over a small child with a camera in his pudgy little hands, was heading toward Artie and company.

Jerry got up on his feet. He dug his hand in the box of popcorn and took out a fistful of buttery puffs.

"Make sure you don't trip, BEEBEEEEE!" Jerry dragged the "E" out for what felt like forever, then he launched his popcorn-filled hand at the mascot, showering it in yellow rain.

Beebee, seemingly forgetting where he was, started rushing up the bleachers at Jerry, pushing families out of his way with his massive cartoon hands.

Artie's bark reached a crescendo as he leapt from his seat. He darted at Beebee, but when he landed on the next bleacher seat going down, he collapsed and let out a whimper.

"Artie!" Tommy yelled.

Scrambling around the people seated in front of him, Tommy reached out and picked up his four-legged friend.

Artie was shaking.

"Artie?"

Everyone, including Beebee, froze.

"What's wrong with him?" Justin asked, visibly concerned.

"I don't know," Tommy said, clutching Artie to his chest. "Grab my bike. Hurry!"

SEVEN

T he ride from the Bandits game was one Tommy would never forget. And thank God for his paper route; the milk crate attached to the front of his bike to hold the papers was the perfect size to fit Artie in, whether he was standing on its edges during a glorious ride or rolled up in a ball like now. Tommy raced from the ballpark to the other side of town to Dr. Finney, the veterinarian he had been taking Artie to since he was a puppy.

Artie sat in the crate as Tommy quickly pedaled, glancing at Tommy with eyes that looked more worried about the boy steering the bicycle than the viewer they belonged to. The bandana that had looked so good on him before had become crooked and wrinkled.

Artie was still shaking and Tommy could tell he was becoming weaker by the way he rested his head on the edge of the crate.

Tommy pedaled as fast as he could. His friends were going to follow but Tommy couldn't wait for them. The chains on his beat-up red bike clicked and clacked. Each time he pushed the pedals down he could feel his heart beat faster and faster.

Night was beginning to creep over the mellow evening and

Dr. Finney's office was about to close. As long as Tommy didn't slow down, he still had a chance to make it there in time.

"Hang on, Art."

Tommy and Artie whipped around the corner of Tessle Street on the red bike and into the veterinarian's parking lot. Some of the security lights inside had already been turned on as the sky melted from beautiful pink hues to a smear of ominous dark purple.

Tommy scooped Artie up from the milk crate. He could feel a chill coming from the little guy as he shook in Tommy's arms.

Tommy ran up the steps to the maroon-colored building, struggled to open the door with one hand while holding Artie, and finally got it to stay open by kicking his foot in the doorway and wedging it open.

"Is Dr. Finney here?" he yelled.

The waiting room was quiet and empty, save for the girl working behind the counter texting on her phone.

She jumped, startled. "What's wrong?" she asked.

Eight

Tommy sat and waited alone in the quiet and cold examination room that Dr. Finney brought him in with Artie. She had calmed Artie down by giving him a small dosage of a sedative so that she could draw blood from him and take him into the room next door for x-rays.

Across from Tommy was Dr. Finney's gray desk where she had a coffee mug that said "Life is better with dogs." Photographs of Dr. Finney's patients were taped along a small shelf on top of the desk: a wiry dachshund in a dog-carrier backpack worn by a pretty girl smiling outside in a park; a golden retriever holding on to a tennis ball that you could tell it loved; an Australian cattle dog, with its unmistakable markings, enjoying life and looking right into the camera, tongue out and right up to the lens.

Tommy thought he had seen that cattle dog around town once before. He was wondering what happened to these animals when the door suddenly opened and Dr. Finney came back into the room. She pushed in a metal table with wheels in front of her. Artie was on it, wrapped in a blanket. His bandana was still tied securely around his neck.

"Here he comes," she said, in a playful voice, the kind doctors must practice to try to lighten stressful situations.

"Is he going to be okay? What's wrong?" Tommy asked.

Artie didn't look like he was going to be okay. Luckily that was mostly because of the sedative that caused him to become groggy and half asleep.

Dr. Finney stopped wheeling the table and let out a huff. She picked a clipboard up off her desk, held it against her chest, and looked at Tommy.

"Tom, how long have you had Artie?" she asked.

"Well, I've always had him," Tommy answered. "We're the same age, thirteen."

"And a lot has happened to you since you've been born, right? You've grown up quite a bit since then. You're not the same little kid you used to be."

"Yeah, I guess so...."

"Think about all of the growing you've done in those thirteen years, and multiply that by, let's say, roughly five. That's how much growing up Artie has done during that time," she said, taking a seat and getting at eye level with Tommy. "Dogs age faster than we do, Tom, and I'm sure you already knew that. So, I'm also sure it's not a big surprise when I tell you that Artie is well into his senior years, which means things are starting to break down on him."

"Break down?" Tommy asked. A sinking feeling of dread pulled at Tommy's insides.

"His blood tests and the x-rays show that his kidneys are beginning to fail," she said, quick and to the point. "At his age, there isn't much we can do other than give him medication. It won't heal him, but it will help with the blood flow to and from the kidneys, prolonging his life and helping to make him more comfortable."

Tommy bit the inside of his lip. He wasn't going to cry, not here at least, but the Arms of Pain were slowly wrapping tightly around him and their partner in crime, the Wall of Time, had come out of nowhere and Tommy had run smack into it, knocking him off his feet. It was that same wall that only appears out of nowhere a few times in your life, telling you that it's time to pay up, no matter if you're ready to or not. There's no way around it.

Tommy looked over at Artie laying on the metal table between him and Dr. Finney. His eyes were fully opened now and he was alert, with a scared expression that hurt Tommy's heart to see.

"How long does he have?" Tommy finally found the courage to ask, beginning to feel a knot in his throat.

"You should know this is late-stage kidney failure. The medication I'll give you will help for now, however ..." Dr. Finney trailed off and gave him a look he could read without the help of her words. There was a hint of compassion behind that look that Tommy wasn't used to seeing from Dr. Finney. Like most doctors, those for people and animals, Dr. Finney usually stayed cold and professional.

"I'm sorry," she said. "He doesn't have long."

"Is there anything else I can do? There has to be."

"Thirteen years is a long time," Dr. Finney said. "Sometimes they can hold on for longer, but once they start getting into their teens it becomes just a matter of luck. Some dogs have it and some dogs don't."

She stood back up.

"If we give him fluid injections that might help, too. They'll also help stabilize his kidneys," she said. "Eventually, though, he's going to begin losing weight and his quality of life won't be the same—*he* won't be the same—and you'll have to make a decision. For now, all you can do is take care of him the best you can, while you can."

Tommy nodded.

He walked over to Artie, who he could tell couldn't wait to go home, and gave him a big hug.

NINE

It had been a long day at work down at the bakery and Jack Balker was happy to finally be pulling into his driveway on Sunfish Lane.

He put his "Macho Man" minivan, as he enjoyed jokingly calling it, into park and was greeted by a scrawny and shirtless ten-year-old redhead boy being chased through a sprinkler by a black Labrador retriever.

"Home sweet home," Jack said, unbuckling his seat belt and reaching over to the passenger seat for leftover cupcakes. Being a baker wasn't the most glorious job in the world, or the highest paying. The days he was able to bring surprises back home to his son, Sam, more than made up for it.

The shirtless Sam ran up to the minivan as Jack got out.

"Whatcha got today, Dad?" he asked behind a mat of wet hair covering his eyes. His freckles beamed with his curiosity.

"One-day-old peanut butter and chocolate cupcakes baked by yours truly. Think your mom will like them?"

"She hates peanut butter."

"I know. That's why I brought them home so we can have them," Jack said, chuckling.

Sam started jumping up and down, like all children do when

there's a treat in front of them that's out of reach. His canine comrade, Milo, watched in excitement and started copying him.

"Can I have one now?" Sam asked.

"You trying to make me have to sleep on the couch tonight?"

Jack ruffled Sam's wet hair and headed for the front door of the house.

It was a nice-looking two-story Cape-style house colored yellow with white framing.

Trees lined the sides of its yard instead of neighbors' houses, which was exactly why Jack and his wife Lindsey picked it and moved in the previous year, despite it having numerous problems from having been abandoned for almost four years. Privacy was what they were looking for, and they had found it here. Their backyard was safe from any prying eyes, surrounded by a forest that went on and on, as far as Jack knew. He also knew that he needed to fix the cracked outside light that was flickering on and off due to water getting into it from the broken gutter above. The house was still a work in progress, if you asked him. Nevertheless, it was home all the same.

"You and Milo come back inside before dark," he said. "And make sure you two dry off. If you come into the house wet like a fish, I'll never hear the end of it."

"Okay, Dad! Don't eat all the cupcakes without me!"

"I'll try not to," Jack said, smiling. "No promises."

Sam went back to playing with Milo and Jack headed inside, cursing under his breath at the leaky gutter.

TEN

As it turned out, Jack still ended up sleeping on the couch because Milo got ahold of the cupcakes and ate all of them.

Milo's dessert didn't sit well with his stomach, giving him constant diarrhea. He had to be brought outside over and over again so he wouldn't have an accident in the house.

God forbid anything gets on the rug, Jack thought to himself with a sting of annoyance, thinking of his wife's adoration for the oriental rug she purchased at Carpet Emporium downtown.

Jack was tired and had been hoping for a good night's sleep, but between Lindsey's aggravation at him for not keeping an eye on the cupcakes and the fact that he could get Milo outside quicker from the living room to take care of his business, he decided to shack up with the Labrador on the couch.

After all, a little alone time with the pooch wasn't so bad. He hardly got to see Milo because he worked so much, and he reminded Jack of the black Labrador he had when he was growing up. That was, in part, some of the reason why he selfishly insisted on getting him for Sam in the first place.

No brothers or sisters? That's nothing good ol' Milo couldn't fix. And he had. He and Sam had become close since Jack first picked the rescue puppy up for adoption two years prior, and it warmed his heart to see it.

"How's he doing?"

Jack jerked awake. He had nodded off in between trips outside. Sam, on the other hand, hadn't. He was wide awake and standing halfway down the staircase in his comic book Flash PJs. He looked worried.

"He'll be fine, son. We'll take him to the vet tomorrow if it keeps up. Right now, let's just let him be."

"Okay."

Sam walked the rest of the way down the stairs and over to where Milo was sleeping on the couch next to Jack. He leaned over and gave his dog a hug.

"Sorry your tummy is hurting you, Milo," he said to him. "We'll make it better. I promise."

Milo stirred as if to wake up, but simply yawned without opening his eyes. Sam gave him another hug, kissed him between the eyes, and headed back up the stairs.

ELEVEN

The late-night talk shows were finished and the infomercials of the wee hours of the morning had begun. Jack had fallen asleep with the TV on, basked in its glow while darkness made itself at home in the rest of the house.

A pencil-thin man with a long, narrow face and slicked-back hair was trying to sell Jack a cleaning kit for a pool he didn't own.

"One run through with Super Powered Magic Glow and your pool will be the envy of all your neighbors!" the stickman said with a wide, bright smile that suggested maybe the product wasn't only limited to pools.

Milo woke up and pawed at Jack's shoulder, nudging him slowly from sleep.

"What is it? You need to go out again?" Jack asked the dog.

Milo gave a whimper that meant yes, he needed to go out and he needed to go out pronto. Jack got up and put on his slippers. Walking to the sliding-glass door in the kitchen, he noticed a faint red glow coming from the woods in the backyard. He rubbed the sleep out of his eyes and when he looked again the glow was gone.

He grabbed Milo's orange leash and hooked it onto his red collar.

"Make this quick, buddy."

Jack stepped outside onto the back deck and into the empty night with his son's dog. It was warm, but with a tinge of damp coolness that never really seems to leave New England no matter what time of the year it is.

The house's outside light lit up the deck like a flickering spotlight, fading into black the farther away you walked from it and into the rest of the yard. It was a small backyard surrounded by those seemingly never-ending woods. The short, white-picket fence Jack started to put up around it was only halfway complete. He didn't like taking Milo out here at night after hearing stories about coyotes moving into the area. Someone in Pebble Falls, the next town over, claimed just a month prior that one scooped up their puppy and ate it. No one had seen a coyote in that town before or since that incident.

Jack and Milo stepped down from the deck with the Labrador leading the way. He was sniffing around, starting toward his usual spot near the bird bath until he took a sharp left in the direction of the woods.

"Milo, c'mon, not that way," Jack said, tugging at his collar with the leash.

Milo had picked up the scent of something and wasn't giving an inch.

"Milo!"

Although the Lab wasn't fully grown yet, he already had strength that matched Jack's. Milo pulled them both toward the woods, taking them just barely on the outskirts of the flickering light.

"Milo, get over here!" Jack yelled in a don't-want-to-wake-the-neighbors kind of way.

Milo didn't listen, and that's when Jack saw it again. The red glow in the woods, this time closer. It was a circle shape far away in between the trees, growing taller and wider.

The thought of Little Red Riding Hood passed through Jack's mind.

He squinted his eyes as the glow became brighter, closer.

"What in the world?"

Milo perked his head up at the moving shape. It was coming at them.

"Milo ..."

Milo started to growl. The woods suddenly became painted in a red neon glow.

Jack stared at it, awestruck and in disbelief. He squinted harder, trying to look deeper into the light burning his eyes and what was in its center. What he saw next he couldn't comprehend. He felt hopeless and shackled by surprising fear. Milo saw it too, and showed it his teeth. With a snarl, he lunged in its direction, pulling the leash out of Jack's hands. Jack felt the last bit of the leash's fabric escape from him before he could snap back to reality.

"Milo! No!" he yelled in a let's-wake-the-neighbors kind of way.

Sam, nestled safely in his bed and dreaming, woke up.

TWELVE

The next evening, the neighbors of Sunfish Lane decided to have a meeting at Carl Crocker's house. Or, put more accurately, Mr. Crocker called a meeting to try and calm the nerves of his neighbors.

Carl Crocker was the unofficial neighborhood "sheriff" and was the one who stuck the neighborhood watch signs at both ends of the road, with one featured in the center of the cul-de-sac. He was good at his job and the people of Sunfish Lane trusted him. When the Barrys' home had been broken into while they were on vacation in Europe (a very rare occurrence of crime in an area that had very little), Crocker was the one who noticed the adolescent thieves jumping their fence and called the police, making good on his signs, you could say. And when old Ms. Lowe fell and broke her hip, Crocker—with his big, handsome smile—was the first one to visit her in the hospital with flowers and check up on her when she returned home. He was, all in all, the perfect neighbor. The kind you wished you had but never seemed to get.

After his wife, Deborah, passed from ovarian cancer six months prior, the sixty-year-old Crocker—with his helmet of perfectly brushed hair—had begun taking an interest in the well-being of others. It helped him take his mind off that goddamn cancer they call the Silent Killer.

True to its name, it snuck up on Deborah and Carl Crocker, and it snuck up fast. Before Crocker knew it, Deborah was gone, and he was left alone for the first time in over three decades. He had been in shambles, slowly piecing himself back together ever since.

"Okay, everyone. One at a time," he said.

His living room was packed and everyone was talking at once, even the usually quiet and feeble Mr. Corn.

"Carl, what are you going to do about this?" asked the elderly Corn. "I have two cats that enjoy their freedom outdoors but I don't dare let them out now."

"Forget about your cats! What about my poor Mrs. Skittles?" cried Evelynn Crofton from her seat on the sofa. She had made herself right at home, taking up a good portion of the flower-embroidered furniture with a front row seat to the cheese plate Crocker had put together.

He's such a great host, she thought to herself as she sampled the Swiss. *And mighty good looking in that white polo shirt, too.*

"Please, I can't hear any of you if you all keep talking over each other," Crocker said, waving a hand in the air. "I understand that there has been quite a scare in our neck of the woods lately and I've asked all of you here tonight so we can talk about it in a calm and orderly fashion."

"This ain't no television show so don't be spewin' any speeches at me, Crocker," said Mr. Corn.

Crocker laughed, taking Mr. Corn's warning lightly.

"I don't want to be delivering any speeches either, Mr. Corn," Crocker said. "God knows, I'm not the one for that. What I want is to hear about what anyone has seen or heard recently that struck them as strange. As you know, Ms. Crofton here and the Balkers have experienced tragedy as it pertains to their four-legged loved ones, and there is growing concern and speculation about what exactly has happened."

"And what *exactly* has happened?" asked Mrs. Jokowski, snarky middle-aged mother of two.

"Well," said Crocker, placing his hands on his hips. "We don't exactly know."

"Don't know?" said Mr. Corn, with more than a hint of sarcasm.

"Mrs. Skittles," Evelynn interrupted, cheese in mouth. "They tore her head off! Tore it off!" she screamed, as if suddenly remembering the whole incident all over again.

The gray-haired Mrs. Dwyer put her arms around Evelynn's shoulders and whispered something in her ear. Whatever she said worked and Evelynn went back to enjoying her cheese.

"Yes, and we're all very sorry about Mrs. Skittles," said Crocker. He paused for a moment, looking down at his feet as if having an unannounced moment of silence.

He looked back up and continued.

"Last night the Balkers experienced something they can't quite explain and have lost their dog Milo as a result."

"Lost, as in torn to shreds like Mr. Skittles?" asked George Farrison, a bald, black man who used to be a security guard at the ferry terminal downtown (it seemed he and Jerry Redman got their news from the same reputable source).

"*Mrs.* Skittles!" Evelynn shouted, correcting Farrison and crying all over again.

"No, Milo has gone missing," said Crocker. "The family wanted me to ask all of you to keep an eye out for him. He's a black Lab."

"So, what's with all this strange talk, Crocker?" asked Mr. Corn. "There's something you're not telling us."

Crocker looked at everyone, assessing the situation and realizing he better just tell them.

"Jack Balker told me that he had brought Milo out into his backyard last night and saw something."

"I bet it's those damn coyotes," Mrs. Jokowski said.

Crocker shook his head.

Mr. Corn leaned forward on his cane. This was getting good.

"Saw what?" asked Mr. Corn, eyes widening.

"A light. Some sort of bright red light coming from the woods. He got distracted by it and that's when Milo took off and ran at it."

Mr. Corn's bushy eyebrows narrowed down to a point that looked like the levers on a pinball machine.

"You pulling my leg, Crocker? You pulling *our* legs?"

Everyone started talking at the same time again, and much louder than before.

"You expect us to believe in UFOs, Mr. Crocker?" Mrs. Jokowski chimed in. She had an expression of disgust on her face.

Carl Crocker shook his head again, trying to keep his cool. He could tell he was starting to lose them and the team-up of Mr. Corn and Mrs. Jokowski was beginning to rub him the wrong way.

"I'm not talking about UFOs. The problem, to be totally honest with you, is that I don't know what I'm talking about or what we're dealing with here," he said. "It very well could be coyotes, but we have no way of telling for sure. The authorities are fully aware of the situation. The problem is that without any leads they can't really help us. Other than the occasional drive-by they make on their nightly rounds, we can't expect much more from them. Because of that, I've decided to take it upon myself to do my own nightly watch and implement an 8 P.M. curfew every evening until we all feel safe again."

"A nightly watch, huh? Sunfish Lane's own personal security guard," said George Farrison, thinking of his long nights on the docks where nothing ever happened. "You know I—"

"Mr. Farrison I know exactly what you're going to say, but rest assured I can handle it. You don't have to worry about a thing."

Judy Simmons, a skinny woman whose frazzled, stuck up black hair would make the bride of Frankenstein look twice, jumped from her seat.

"Oh, Mr. Crocker! You would do that for us?" she said, sounding almost turned on by the idea. Judy had been sitting quietly on the red love seat, listening intently to Crocker's words with the honed-in concentration of a teeny bopper watching Elvis Presley swivel his hips on stage. If the fact that she was alone and baked him a pie for every holiday wasn't enough of a clue, she had a slight infatuation with the man in the white polo shirt.

Crocker knew. Especially now, looking at her hypnotized eyes.

"Of course, Judy," he said. "As your neighborhood leader, I feel terrible about what's going on right now in our little oasis. Mr. Corn can't let his cats out, the Balkers' dog is missing, and I don't want to begin trying to imagine what could happen next."

"And Mrs. Skittles!" cried Evelynn, again.

"And Mrs. Skittles," he reassured her.

"You keep an extra eye on that quack Mr. Rooney," Evelynn said.

"I'm not going to single out one person unless I suspect with absolute certainty that there's a reason to," he said. Then, with that Crocker smile, "I plan on being equally nosy on all of you. Anyway, what else is a retired guy to do?"

The group of Sunfish Lane neighbors broke out in laughter and began to clap, even Mr. Corn and Mrs. Jokowski joined in. Smiles stretched from wall to wall in Crocker's cramped living room as each of his neighbors let out all of their nervous energy.

Carl Crocker smiled right back at them.

He would save them.

Of course he would.

THIRTEEN

The clicker for the television wasn't working again and Ronald Rooney was getting fed up. He had the same clicker for so long that he was beginning to think it wasn't just the batteries that were giving up on him. Maybe Old Man Rooney—as the neighborhood kids liked to call him behind his back, and some of the adults, if we're being honest—had an old clicker to match his nickname.

Heh. That's what happens when you get your buttons pushed too many times, he thought to himself.

He wasn't completely unaware of what the others in the neighborhood made of him. It was hard not to be when every time he passed Evelynn the Elephant's house she'd give him a dirty look and slam the door with her cat in hand.

Damn cat.

Those were the days when he used to go on walks around the neighborhood.

But it had been almost ten years since he stepped off his front deck, never wanting to leave his abode since that terrible wreck on the highway on the way back with his wife Helen from their annual anniversary dinner at Leo's Italian Restaurant. That's what losing your wife of 42 years will do to you; that's what having a stroke will do to you, too, he supposed. Add the physical pain of an annoying limp with the mental stress and guilt of being the one who survived the crash, and you're left with the perfect cocktail of misery.

There was another guilt that plagued the old man, too. One buried deeper in his past.

Thank heavens for the boob tube and the meds. And online shopping, for that matter. Once he figured out how to boot the computer up and navigate that pesky arrow, Old Man Rooney had no reason to leave the house. Groceries and just about everything else under the sun could be conveniently delivered right to his doorstep without him even having to brush his hair, or what remained of it.

He wasn't always Old Man Rooney. There was a time—long before little arrows on a screen that didn't go where you wanted them to—when this crippled old soul was a vibrant blast of energy, practicing medicine during the day at his office and in the evenings pulling his boat of a Chevy up to the same house he was in now. Except back then there was a beautiful new bride and a baby waiting for him inside that didn't despise him. These days he's surrounded by boxes of photos he pulled out of the closet and never bothered to put back.

And fish tanks. Lots and lots of fish tanks.

It had started out as a hobby for him to help take his mind off of things. Before he knew it, he had ten fish tanks scattered all around the house. One large tank that was five feet long took over the living room. He liked to keep small, brightly colored neon tetra because they were easy to take care of and fun to watch. He must have had a few dozen of them scattered between some of the tanks. He also had some platy fish and guppies. His angelfish, which he kept in the living room, were his favorite. Old Man Rooney would sit there, dazed by their majestic maneuvers as they glided around the surrounding neon tetra they shared the tank with.

Most of the tanks were empty, though, save for the water. The fish in those had died and Old Man Rooney couldn't order anymore from Pet Party because the local business recently went into foreclosure and was no longer delivering. What he would do when all his fish had died and he was left with none and no way to get any more was a worry he tried to push into the basement of his head, along with a great many other things. That was okay; he still had just enough to keep him company for the time being.

Today, however, not even his angelfish could calm his mind.

"This goddamn clicker!" he yelled, tossing the television remote across the room where it hit the wall and dropped to the ground with all the grace of a swatted fly.

He went to pick it up and looked out the window.

"Not again. Come on, kid."

Tommy was outside delivering the *Brighton Falls Gazette*. It was his first job ever, one that he picked up as a summertime gig and had already started before the end of the school year.

Luckily classes didn't start until 8 A.M. so he was able to get the papers delivered before homeroom. More importantly, it was helping fund the medication Artie now needed. All he had to do was hop on his bike, ride up and down the street, and make sure he didn't hit anyone with the paper when he threw it. He kept the satchel for the papers over his shoulder to make room for Artie in the milk crate attached to the front of the bike.

Artie loved to ride. Although he was sick, he still lifted his head up in the air, catching the breeze as they rode together, like the captain of a ship leading the way. His big white ears with their brown markings flapped in the wind and he would turn to look back at Tommy, his co-captain.

Tommy swore Artie was smiling every time he did this.

Rooney swung his screen door open and let it close with a loud *CLAP*. He clumsily made his way down the first two steps of the deck with his cane in an awkward hurry. He came to an abrupt stop when he reached the third and final step, teetering on its edge and almost falling over.

His house was on a big hill, from which, if you looked out east from the window on its top floor, you could see the entire neighborhood below. To the west were the woods.

"Hey, kid!" he yelled.

Tommy was pedaling away and was almost to the Westons' house next door when he heard Rooney. He slammed on his brakes.

Oh, no, Tommy thought to himself.

Jerry had said that Old Man Rooney got in trouble one time for kidnapping kids and bringing them back up to his house for devil sacrifices. That's why he never leaves his house, Jerry reasoned, because he worked out a deal with the town to make sure that he would never do it again. Old Man Rooney kept the bones of the kids on display in his house, according to Jerry.

Tommy turned and saw Rooney on his hands and knees on the deck step, stretching out his cane and fishing the paper closer to him with it, avoiding touching the ground as if it was hot lava. He finally got the paper within arm's length and picked it up.

"You see what you've done here?" Rooney said as he held the paper up in the air with his left hand and used his right to prop himself back up with the cane. "You're new, so I'm going to give you a break, but you can't just toss my *Gazette* in the yard."

Tommy couldn't see Rooney's lips moving behind his straggly white beard, but they were certainly getting a workout in.

Rooney lifted his cane and pointed it at Tommy. The cane looked carved and handmade. Instead of being flat and smooth, the dark mahogany wood had dips and crevices like a choppy ocean.

"You gotta get it on the deck," he said, out of breath and pushing the tip of the cane at Tommy at the end of each word for added emphasis. He looked like he was about to tip over and be boiled in his imaginary lava.

"You gotta—"

RRRRAAARR!!!

Artie dashed from the milk crate and up the hill directly at the old man. The cane-wielding senior citizen froze with surprise before changing his target to Artie, jabbing the cane at the beagle in a desperate attempt to fend him off. Artie wasn't having it. He grabbed the business end of Old Man Rooney's weapon with his mouth and pulled at it.

For a moment, Tommy stood there and watched in awe at this slightly humorous power struggle. Here was Old Man Rooney, hermit extraordinaire, outside in his green bathrobe and mad scientist hair standing on end, fighting with Artie. Flashbacks of their encounter with Evelynn Crofton came back to him.

"You mutt! Get him off!" Old Man Rooney yelled. He was losing his balance and going to fall.

"Artie, let go. It's okay," Tommy called out.

Artie had no plans of letting go, not as long as this madman was still heckling them. He was clamped down hard.

Tommy ran over and wrapped his arms around Artie and rubbed his belly.

He whispered in his ear, "Art, let's go."

Artie, with his bite still locked on the cane, turned his big brown eyes up to Tommy without letting go.

"Artie."

Slowly, the beagle lightened his grip and his tense little body began to relax. Old Man Rooney yanked his cane free and slammed it into the deck step, getting his balance back.

"I should call animal control! That dog attacked me!"

"He wasn't attacking you. He was just trying to protect me."

"I don't care how you try to sugarcoat it. If I had two good feet ..."

"Come on, Art," Tommy said, picking the dog up. He walked Artie back to the bike and placed him back inside the milk crate. Tommy patted his head and Artie seemed to enjoy it, but not before giving Rooney one last look for good measure.

"Pedal away, you little squirt," said Rooney, still catching his breath. "And don't forget what I said about my paper."

And Tommy did just that, pedaling the rest of the way down

Sunfish Lane and delivering the last few papers he had left for that morning's run before heading to homeroom for the final day of school. He made sure Old Man Rooney got his paper on his deck from then on, too.

Fourteen

Lindsey wasn't expecting company, so when she heard the knock on her front door she jumped. She hadn't a chance to take her spaghetti lunch out of the microwave yet and was already in a hurry to get back to work before her break was over. Working at the post office nearby in town had its benefits, and taking her half-hour break at home was one of them.

The visitor knocked on the door again, slightly louder this time.

"Hold on," Lindsey said with a hint of irritation.

Did Jack schedule the cable guy or something? she wondered. *I really wish he would tell me these things.*

She threw down the towel she was using to wipe spaghetti sauce off her hands and headed for the door, gearing herself up to take her Jack-anger out on the unsuspecting cable guy.

She grabbed the door handle, clenched it and pulled.

A nervous smile broke out on her face. "Oh, hi."

"Hello there, Mrs. Balker. How do you do?"

Carl Crocker, in all his neighborly glory, stood in Lindsey's doorway with a calm poise and friendly smile. The yellow polo he was wearing was perfect for the sunny day behind him.

"I'm—I'm fine, Carl. What brings you here?" Lindsey stuttered.

"May I come in?"

"Oh, sure. Of course."

Crocker stepped inside and took a look around, his attention directed toward the humming microwave in the kitchen. Lindsey saw this and her hand went involuntarily to her mouth, checking to make sure there wasn't any leftover spaghetti sauce on her lips from the portion she had sampled.

"I hope I'm not interrupting anything."

"No, no, I'm just on lunch break," she said, cutting in front of him on her way to the kitchen and shutting the microwave off even though it wasn't finished heating up her food.

"Can I get you some water or juice?" she asked.

"That's not necessary. I'm here because from what I understand you still haven't been able to find your dog. Is that right?"

Lindsey's gaze lowered and she turned to the window looking out on the backyard.

"Yes, unfortunately there hasn't been any sign of him since Jack took him out that night."

"I'm sorry to hear that. Tough on your son, I'm sure."

Crocker leaned down and peered out the sliding-glass door as if something caught his eye. "Is Jack home now? I'd love to speak with him in person. We only had a chance to talk briefly on the phone."

"No, he's still at work. He hasn't been taking it too well, either. He's been acting rather strange since that night, to be honest. But he could probably help you more than I can. He saw whatever it is he claims is out there," Lindsey answered, with more than a spit of spite and embarrassment directed at her husband.

Crocker's eyes shifted back over to Lindsey. "Strange? How?"

"I'm not really sure. I'm probably just overreacting. You're welcome to come back later when he's here if you want to talk with him about it. I know you've taken the initiative to keep an eye out for us with everything going on lately, and we all really appreciate it."

Crocker straightened himself back up and put his hands on his hips.

"Well, I'm not trying to get in the way of the police, but sometimes those boys in blue have their hands full and a little neighborhood camaraderie can go a long way."

Lindsey's smile returned. "I suppose so."

Like a magnetic force field, Crocker returned his attention to the backyard through the glass door. "Mind if I poke around? Maybe my fresh eyes can spot something Jackie boy missed."

"Um, sure, go ahead. I have to go back to work, so—"

Crocker showed her his big grin and for a moment, maybe two, Lindsey felt in love.

"That's fine. You go right along back to work. I can let myself out through the side of the yard. If I find anything worth finding, I'll be sure to let you guys know one way or another."

With that, Crocker slid the sliding-glass door open and stepped onto the deck, leaving Lindsey with her half-heated spaghetti and a flutter in her heart.

FIFTEEN

Some of Milo's toys were still scattered on the deck and Crocker almost tripped over a purple one shaped like a T-rex. A dash of temper took over him and he quickly kicked the toy out of the way. He glanced over his shoulder to see if Lindsey was watching. She wasn't. She must have already left, and that was good. No, better than good; it was super-duper good.

He stepped down off the deck and surveyed the area, looking like he knew exactly what he wanted. His scope continued past the bird feeder where Milo had peed so many times before. Crocker approached the border of where the neatly kept grass of the backyard met the mashup of straggly forest grass and gray, broken twigs. He walked through the divide, past the incomplete fence Jack had started. The fence abruptly ended like an unfinished story and left a clear opening, a doorway from the civilized world to the wild. Things might have turned out much differently for poor Milo if Jack had just finished putting up the fence, Crocker thought to himself.

Crocker made his way past the small brush and into the deepening woods. He moved branches out of his way with both of his arms. He saw something up ahead that made him pause and his eyes widen. He picked up his pace and disappeared into the green canvas behind the Balkers' home.

SIXTEEN

I t was the last day of school at Brighton Falls Middle School and you could tell by the lack of control the teachers had over the students; someone had taken toilet paper and ceremoniously covered the stairwell, while someone else decided to take red paint from the art room and write "Mrs. Tobey has big boobs" across the cafeteria wall.

The beginning of summer waited on the other side of the school doors. For Tommy and his friends, they couldn't wait for the final bell to ring so they could escape from Ms. Tierney's English class for the next two and a half months.

"Okay, I say we hit up Sal's Market first to get some ice cream then we hang outside until Sarah Lackey and the rest of her friends walk by," Jerry said, leaning over a copy of *The Old Man and the Sea*. They had been assigned to read the book for summer reading and Ms. Tierney was graciously giving them a head start.

"Why don't you just go talk to her right now?" Justin asked.

Sarah Lackey was sitting in the front row, twirling her long brunette hair around her finger and chatting with a girl sitting next to her.

"No, no, no," Jerry answered very matter-of-fact and with a lowered voice. "Not here in this setting. I need to wait."

"What's wrong with this setting?" Justin teased him. "I thought you two were besties?"

Jerry's face turned red. "Yeah, I'd just rather, you know, talk to her without Ms. Tierney yelling at me to be quiet."

"All right then, what happens when we see her at Sal's?"

"You know, look cool."

Eric put his book down. "That's your big plan to get her attention?" he asked. "You're never going to see her belly button again."

"If he ever did," added Justin.

Eric and Justin shared a chuckle, prompting Ms. Tierney to give her obligatory "be quiet and read" look before dozing back off behind her desk.

"What about you, Tommy? You coming with us?" asked Jerry.

Tommy, who was actually trying to read the book, put it down. "Sorry, guys. I have to head home and give Artie his medicine."

"How's ol' Artie doing?" asked Justin.

"He's hanging in there," Tommy said, trying to sound positive. "Just can't miss giving him any of his medication. He's on a pretty tight schedule."

"You do what you gotta do for him and we'll catch up later," said Eric. "We won't be up to much anyway, especially if we keep listening to Jerry over here."

"Hey, don't be mad at me that the only belly button you have a shot at seeing is your secret admirer's," Jerry said, pointing to Ms. Tierney.

"Jerry, I swear I'm gonna—" Eric started, and then the bell rang.

It was here, finally: summer vacation.

Jerry closed his book with a quick *SNAP* and threw it in his bag where it would remain unread for the rest of the summer. Eric and Justin did the same as everyone jumped from their desk and bolted for the door.

Ms. Tierney broke out of her sleep. "Don't forget once you finish reading you have to write a two-page summary of your thoughts about the story," she said. "And I mean *your* thoughts! Not some reviewer's you copied online!"

More than half the students were already out the door, thoughts about an old man fishing the last thing on their mind.

"And have a good summer," She trailed off.

Justin, Jerry, and Eric slung their backpacks over their shoulders, three musketeers ready for the glory of summer.

"Later, Tommy. We'll be at Sal's if you decide to come," Jerry said, with one foot out the door.

"I'll see you guys later," Tommy said. He sat by himself for a moment, thinking about how fast life seemed to be moving lately. Sometimes he wished he could just press pause and stop everything from changing. Was he the only one who felt this way? All of his friends seemed to know exactly what they were going to do next and how they wanted to do it. Thoughts like these never crossed his mind just a few years ago. Normally he'd be out the door with everybody else.

Tommy finally zipped up his bag and made his way out the classroom door. He entered the hall and approached the stairs leading to outside, the sound of the last students' cheers echoing through the stairwell as they swung the doors at the bottom open and escaped into the summer. Tommy thought he was the only one left in the building—even Ms. Tierney was gone—but then he heard something that didn't belong in this moment of youthful joy: crying. Sam Balker was sitting on the stairwell with his head in his hands, sobbing. Tommy had a feeling he knew what was wrong.

Sam was always quiet and kept mostly to himself from what Tommy saw. Despite the two being in different grades, Tommy was aware of Sam because they lived in the same neighborhood and occasionally took the same bus. But Tommy had never seen him outside of school or with any friends. He didn't know if Sam even had any friends for that matter. Some of the older kids (the ones who were the same age as Tommy) would pick on him and call him Sweaty Sam because he'd sweat profusely when he got nervous, which turned out to be quite often. That sort of thing, as silly as it may sound, can damage a kid, and it was already starting to make Sam a loner.

"Hey, Sam, you all right?" Tommy asked, taking a seat next to him on the step.

Sam, startled, leapt from his spot. He thought he was the only one left in the school, too.

He wiped tears from his face, which had become bright red and almost matched his freckles.

"It's your dog, isn't it?" asked Tommy. "Milo. Is that his name?"

Sam nodded.

"He still hasn't come home?"

Word had gotten around, among adults and children alike, about what had happened to the Balkers.

"We don't know if he—" Sam started to choke up again and stopped himself. "We don't know if he ever will. My mom told me not to get my hopes up."

"You've been looking for him though, right?"

"As much as my parents will let me," Sam said. "They don't want me going way back into the woods. I know my dad has gone a couple of times but I've watched him and he never seems to go very far."

It was true. Jack had gone out to look for Milo, and every time he did, he'd be struck by a crippling wave of guilt that froze him. He was afraid of what he'd find in the woods—what he would have to say to his son if he found the lifeless body of his best friend in a damp clump of leaves. And, not that he would admit it, but he didn't want to chance seeing that *thing* again; the sight he refused to talk to his wife about, if, in fact, it was actually real and not his wide-awake imagination playing games with his half-awake mind. He wasn't able to totally make out what it was—the red glow was blinding and by the time it stopped and he could readjust his eyes, Milo and the thing in the woods were both already gone. The parts he did manage to catch a glimpse of, however, rattled his brain. He wished every day since then that he hadn't seen any of it.

"How far is far?" Tommy asked.

"I don't really know," Sam said. "I heard him talk about a drop back there or something. A big hill, I guess, and it just keeps going."

"Well, I don't know about you, but I've got all summer ahead of me and I'm itching for some fresh air. Mind if I tag along with you?" Tommy said.

"I can't. My parents don't want me going out there."

Tommy didn't doubt that Sam's parents didn't want him venturing into the woods. But he could also tell that Sam was scared to go alone.

"They don't want you going out there on your own," Tommy said, smiling. "You won't be alone if I'm with you. Plus, I have a special friend who I think can help us."

SEVENTEEN

The sun hung in the sky with all the promise of a gift waiting to be opened. It was warm without being too hot. Those sweltering days were around the corner. For now, as Tommy made his way to Sam's house on his bike, it was the perfect meeting of late spring and early summer.

Artie sat in his milk carton seat, looking straight ahead with his head held high in the air. His medicine perked him up a little, much to the relief of Tommy. He noticed lately that Artie was beginning to become picky with his food and as a result didn't have his normal amount of energy all the time. Their usual routine of Tommy going into bed every night with Artie jumping up behind him had changed to Artie standing up on his two hind legs and leaning his front legs against the side of the bed, waiting for Tommy to lift him up.

Artie was the one doing the lifting now, boosting Tommy's spirit and making him feel like maybe they could really help Sam find Milo. There weren't any cars in Sam's driveway either, which would also make it easier for the three of them to go into the woods without having to worry about Sam's parents spotting them.

Tommy slowed down and came to a stop at the end of the

driveway. He kicked out the kickstand and took his old and faded blue backpack off.

"Okay, Artie. Let's see if we can bring Milo home."

Tommy unzipped the backpack and placed it on the ground. He gently picked Artie up out of the milk crate and slipped him into the bag, bottom first so that his head was safely poking out from it. Artie sniffed the blue bag, inspecting it the same way he inspected everything. Artie looked at Tommy, slightly confused but still with trust in his eyes.

"That's just so you don't wear yourself out," Tommy said to him. "I'll let you sniff around when we get out there."

Artie blinked, acknowledging Tommy's words.

Tommy put the bag back around his back. It was heavier with Artie in it but he'd rather bear the weight than have Artie strain himself. He kicked the kickstand back up and rolled the bike over to some bushes on the side of Sam's house, hiding it in them just in case his parents came home while they were gone.

The Balkers' house looked better to Tommy than it had in recent years when he rode by it, although he could see it still had remnants left over from its time being unlived in. The side where he placed his bike wasn't painted the same yellow as the rest. Instead, it had plain darkened shingles starting to fall off it. He could also see the rickety fence in the backyard wasn't complete and a gap was left, leading into what must have been the woods Sam spoke of, Tommy thought.

"Hey, Tommy!" Sam yelled from his bedroom window on the second floor, poking his head out and scaring the bejesus out of Tommy. "I'll be right out!" he yelled, and was gone in a flash.

A door could be heard being slammed from inside the house and something came crashing down. The front door to the house flew open and out came Sweaty Sam Balker, already wiping his brow with his arm.

"What's that in your backpack?" he asked, half out of breath.

"Sam, I'd like you to meet a good friend of mine."

EIGHTEEN

The sight of Artie brought a smile to Sam's face, the kind of smile Tommy imagined Milo also gave him. Sam stroked the smooth fur on top of Artie's head poking out of Tommy's backpack. Artie, of course, loved it. He always loved attention.

"This here is Artie," Tommy told Sam.

"Hello, Artie. Nice to meet you."

Artie nudged his nose up as if saying hi.

"He has a great sense of smell," Tommy said. "One time I had put one of his toys that I found in the backyard in my coat pocket and forgot I left it there. Artie managed to smell it out and took it back out himself, tearing a hole through the pocket."

"Wow, he's got that good of a nose?"

"The best. I'm sure if he can find Milo's scent, he'll be able to follow it to him."

Sam, with a radiant sense of hope, agreed, wiping the sweat again from his face. The three of them headed for the backyard by way of the alley of grass between the side of the house and the bushes where Tommy hid his bike—the same way Crocker told Lindsey he'd exit if he needed.

Tommy, Artie, and Sam crossed the backyard and approached the border of the yard and woods on the far side.

"Thanks for coming over," Sam said, taking a deep breath like a diver about to plunge into depths unknown.

"Don't thank me yet," said Tommy.

"You sure we're not going to get into trouble for this? Does your mom know you came over here?" Sam asked.

"No way," Tommy said. "I told her I was going to the movies. That way if she drives by the ballpark and doesn't see me, she won't get suspicious."

"Oh, yeah. Good idea," Sam said, thinking it over.

With Artie in tow in the backpack, Tommy stepped into the woods first. Sam followed close behind. It wasn't hard to walk through in the beginning, mainly just some brush and skinny tree limbs that stretched out annoyingly in the way.

"So, your dad said Milo ran in this direction?" Tommy asked, careful not to let any of the tree limbs whack him in the face, or Artie in the back of his little head. Artie would start to turn around to see where they were going but would move back whenever he saw Tommy lift a branch.

"Yeah, he said he bolted straight through here," Sam said. "I don't know how far he could've gone."

It was strange, Tommy thought to himself, to see Sam outside of school. It always seemed that way whenever he saw someone he associated with the classroom and schoolwork doing something totally different. It was like seeing a twin of that person you didn't know existed. Sure, Sam still had the sweaty sprinkles going, but there was a sense of determination coming from him that Tommy never noticed before at school. And here they were, another school year behind them and another in waiting. But now—right now, in this moment—they were free; free from the unrequested tribulations of growing up; free from teachers, buses and bullies. As long as there was summer, there was hope.

"You see that big broken tree limb on the ground up ahead?" Sam asked. "That's the farthest I've ever gone."

He said this to Tommy, but it was Artie who was facing him.

The tree limb was long and stubborn, at least seven feet long, and blocked their way with no clear route around it. It must have fallen over during a storm, and because no one ever came out here, it was never moved. Tommy tried lifting it up, but it was too heavy. It had belonged to a large, crooked tree next to it that was leaning and close to falling over. Wide knots jutted from its surface like braille. The tree was old, maybe the oldest in those woods.

Sam came over to Tommy's left side and grabbed part of the tree limb. "Let me help."

"On the count of three," Tommy said. "One, two ... three!"

They both lifted at the same time and managed to get it up off the ground. Tommy nodded to his right side and he and Sam pushed it over, getting it slightly out of their way and creating just enough space to get around it. Sam went ahead first and immediately fell to the ground, slipping on something and landing hard on his back. He let out a loud *OOMPH.*

"Sam!" Tommy yelled.

Sam twisted and squirmed, trying to get back up. Tommy reached out and gave him a hand. Sam got back on his feet and looked at his arms in disgust; there was some sort of thick orange substance all over his arms and legs that almost matched the color of his hair.

"Get it off me! Get it off me!" he shouted, quickly scraping it off like a person with arachnophobia seeing a spider crawling on them.

"What the hell is that?" asked Tommy. "Looks like the inside of a pumpkin."

"Did I get all of it?" Sam asked, on the verge of tears.

Tommy checked. "Most of it," he said, wiping some off of Sam's shoulder.

Tommy hunkered down to get a closer look at the strange substance on the ground and Artie craned his neck around to also take a peek. There was a large heap of it neither one of them had seen under where the tree limb had been. Tommy broke a branch off a nearby tree and poked at the substance, stretching it up slowly to get a good look. It was moist and gooey but beginning to dry up, as if it had been left outside for a long time past its expiration date. The wet portions of it glistened in the sun with pieces of dirt stuck in it protruding out. The branch Tommy was holding snapped under its weight.

Sam was still wiping globs of it off his arms when Tommy stood back up.

"I don't think you have anything to worry about," he said. "Seems harmless."

"I hope so," Sam said, still checking himself. "Pieces of it are still on me. Stuff smells like—"

"Look," Tommy said, pointing ahead the same way a pioneer might with a mix of fear and excitement upon finding new land.

It was a trail, a dirt path just barely visible under the brush and mess Mother Nature made in this forgotten area of Brighton Falls.

"You don't know where that leads to, do you?" Tommy asked.

"I didn't even know it was here," Sam said.

Stringy strands of the orange gunk that tripped Sam were spread across the trail, more than enough to pique a young boy's curiosity.

Tommy tightened his backpack's straps over his shoulders and held on to them. "Then let's find out."

Nineteen

About ten minutes into following the trail, both it and the orange ooze disappeared. The trail seemed to have vanished and been eaten up by the woods like it didn't want to be found.

The ooze came to an abrupt stop. Some outlines of it could be seen on the grass as if it had been removed. The area it led them to was vast and before Tommy knew it, Sam's house was no longer anywhere in sight.

"Milo!" Sam yelled, looking around. His voice carried through the maze of trees. He turned back to Tommy. "I think we've hit a dead end."

"Not yet," Tommy said.

Tommy peeled the straps of his backpack off and placed it gently on the ground. Artie's head stuck out. His eyes locked on Tommy with eager anticipation.

"You up to this, buddy?" he asked the dog.

Artie blinked and opened his mouth with the same expression Tommy always saw whenever he took Artie's toys out.

Tommy smiled. "Okay, then."

He rolled back the zippers that kept Artie securely snug in the bag and reached in it, placed his hands underneath the beagle's armpits, and lifted him out. Artie stood at attention like a soldier waiting for his orders.

"Did you bring what I told you?" Tommy asked Sam.

"Sure did," Sam said, pulling Milo's purple T-rex out of his pocket. "His favorite."

"Great."

Sam handed it to Tommy and Tommy placed the chewed-up dinosaur in front of Artie. The dog smelled it curiously.

Tommy then picked up the last bit of orange gunk and placed it in front of Artie's nose. The beagle's brown and white spotted ears perked up immediately. He lowered his head and carefully sniffed at the foreign substance.

"You think you can find it?" Tommy asked him.

Artie looked back at him with those knowing eyes.

"All right, Artie! Go! Go!"

Artie shot from his sitting stance, rocketing past Sam.

"Where's he going?" Sam asked, whirling around, confused.

Tommy swung his bag back around his shoulders. "To find Milo! Let's go!"

Tommy took off after Artie, trying to keep him in sight. The constant barrage of tree limbs and uneven ground didn't make it easy to run. Sam did his best to keep up while simultaneously checking to make sure he wasn't stepping in anymore of the orange stuff.

The round, hustling white blur up ahead that was Artie bounded up and down, side to side. Tommy couldn't help but feel happy seeing him so full of life despite being sick. "That a boy, Art!" he yelled as he ran.

He closed his eyes for a second when the bristles of a branch poked him in the face. When he opened them back up, Artie was nowhere to be seen.

Tommy came to a stop. "Artie!"

Awhoooo!!!

Artie's howl, long and blue, tunneled through the silence of the woods.

"I'm coming! Hold on!" Tommy answered, picking his speed back up. He wasn't sure where exactly Sam was. He could hear twigs snapping somewhere behind him and figured he wasn't too far away. Tommy wanted Artie back in his sights as soon as possible.

The heavy enclave of tree branches started to finally thin out and Tommy thought he could see an opening beginning to appear. Although overgrown and forgotten, the path led to something. Between the green, he could see the shape of Artie again, his tail wagging excitedly. Tommy let out a sigh of relief. He made his way out of the woods and into a small, round clearing.

Artie started to bark.

TWENTY

Tommy couldn't make out what it was at first. He couldn't catch his breath, either, putting his hands on his knees and gasping for air.

Artie didn't care. He kept barking at the structure in front of him, or what was left of it, sensing not to trust it.

"All right, I hear ya," Tommy said. "I didn't know you could still run like that."

Artie continued to pay Tommy no mind. Instead, he kept his brown eyes locked on the jumble of gray stones in front of him. Tommy straightened his back and turned his focus to what Artie was barking at.

"What'd you find, Art?"

Tommy slowly walked toward what at first looked like a misshapen pile of medium-sized rocks, probably five to ten pounds each. The closer he got to it, it was clear that they weren't just thrown together; they were actually organized into a short circle standing roughly three feet tall. A tangle of green and brown vines had grown up the sides of the short edifice and some of the stones had fallen out of place. The overgrowth stretched across the top of the roughly five-foot-wide circle, covering some of it, but an opening had been made—or torn—through it.

Tommy leaned over the opening in the ground and Artie barked again, this time deeper and with a hint of a growl about to start. Tommy tried to look inside of it. All he saw was darkness.

"What's that?"

Tommy jumped. Sam stood behind him, covered in branches and red marks.

"Is it Milo? Is Milo in there?!"

Tommy shook his head. "I don't know. I just—"

Sam ran at the stone structure, not hearing Tommy. "Milo!"

Sam came up to the edge and placed his hands on the top stones with force, leaning forward and looking into the opening. As soon as he did, the rocks beneath his hands gave way and Sam lost his balance. Tommy tried to grab his arm but missed and got a piece of his t-shirt instead. The remaining vines covering the top of the structure didn't stop Sam's fall like Tommy hoped. Instead, Sam tumbled forward and right through them.

The straggly vines ripped with an unforgiving tear, pulling more stones from the sides and revealing a dark abyss that the rocks fell into. The sound of the falling rocks could be heard echoing off the sides of the tunnel digging into the earth, ultimately landing somewhere far below.

Tommy's grip on Sam's shirt prevented him from falling all the way down, putting Sam in an awkward position of hanging inside the middle of the tunnel between the fresh air above and a foul odor emanating from the dark underneath his feet.

Sam's shirt was starting to rip and Tommy was about to lose his grip on it. Artie let out a series of loud barks as he ran up alongside Tommy and looked down into the black hole to see what was going on.

"You gotta give me your hand," Tommy said to Sam, struggling to keep himself from falling in.

Sam didn't hear him. He was staring in shock at something below.

Who knows how deep this hole is? Tommy thought to himself, and quickly tried not to guess. He could've sworn he heard the falling rocks land with a splash, but with his heart racing, he couldn't be sure.

"Sam, give me your hand! I can't pull you up by your shirt without it ripping more!"

Sam hung helplessly, a red-headed rag doll left out for the wolves—or wolf. All Tommy could see was the top of his hair. The rest of his body was enveloped by darkness. "Sam, can you hear me? Snap out of it!"

Artie howled and Sam's head swiveled around. He looked up and reached his hand out to Tommy and Tommy gripped it tight. Tommy started pulling Sam up and immediately felt something tug back in a quick jerk. Sam screamed out. It was the kind of reaction that started more like a surprised yelp before quickly turning to startled pain.

"What's wrong?" Tommy asked.

"I don't know! Something's down here!"

Sam began to feel long, slender shapes like wet sticks wrap around his ankle. At first, he thought he might be caught in more vines. When the sensation spread up to his knee and tightened, he knew these weren't any vines at all. These felt like fingers.

A brisk fear set into Sam as a cold wetness seeped through his jean pant leg. Tiny prickles of pain shot into his calf, reminding him of a board with nails he had stepped on by accident while running around barefoot in the yard when his father was trying to put the ill-fated fence up.

Sam screamed and the sound echoed in the tight confines he was trapped in.

"Get me out of here, Tommy!"

"I'm trying! Can you kick free?"

Sam thrashed his free foot, trying to kick whatever was holding him down. The grip on his captured leg squeezed tighter and yanked him downward again. The unbearable sensation of pinching nails sent another wave of claustrophobic pain and he started to cry. He flailed, causing the fabric of his shirt in Tommy's hand to rip more.

The rocks keeping Tommy stable and safe from falling in on top of Sam creaked and budged against the pressure of his weight. With one last gasp of energy, Tommy pulled up one more time, was met with double the force, and fell forward, crashing through the rocks that were fortifying him.

For an instant both Tommy and Sam were free falling, hand in hand, one above the other like a sloppy circus performance, until they suddenly froze in place.

Now something had Tommy's leg. It was Artie.

The beagle latched his mouth on Tommy's pant leg with a vice grip, growling with determination to not let go.

"Artie!" Tommy yelled. "Pull!"

Artie did pull and he got them to move slightly up for a second, but another tug from below moved them back to where they were before. Artie pulled again and this time a rock came falling down. Tommy caught it just as it was about to clock him in the face. He looked down at Sam, who was writhing in pain, and saw something else: an outline, a trace of a silhouette, engulfing the area around Sam's feet.

"Cover your head," Tommy yelled, hearing his voice echo. He chucked the rock at the shape. A loud screech pierced through the tunnel in response. Sam kicked his foot free and the weight pulling him down disappeared.

"Let's get out of here, Art!" Tommy yelled up to his friend.

Artie pulled back with all the force he could muster and lifted the two boys up until Tommy was out and could pull Sam back up the rest of the way.

Sam rolled out, shaking. He and Tommy sat on the ground in silent shock, covered in dirt and sweat. Sam didn't blink, didn't say a word. Tommy saw that his pant leg was ripped—shredded was more like it—with blotches of blood coming through the openings. But the thing that surprised Tommy the most wasn't red, it was orange—the same gloopy substance that led them there was covering Sam's leg and foot with a shiny new coat.

Artie, panting, looked at Tommy with his own sense of worry. Tommy laid his hand across Artie's back and kissed his head.

"Thank you," he told him.

Twenty-One

In the days following the incident in the woods, Tommy could tell Artie's health was getting worse. What happened there had been too much on him, and Tommy couldn't stop beating himself up because of it. It was Tommy's decision to bring him and, in the end, Tommy regretted it. He thought Artie could help them, which he most certainly did, but he never wanted Artie to get involved in anything like the chaos they found in the clearing.

Sam told his parents what he saw and what happened. They asked him who he had gone with, and Sam, not used to keeping secrets, informed them it was Tommy. Sam's mother promptly told him to stay away from Tommy as she cleaned up the cuts on his leg. That's what happens when you run in the woods, she told him. His father didn't bring the hammer down on him as hard. Jack's own guilt over Milo was beginning to bubble over more as the summer settled in and he saw his son at home without his dog to pal around with. Now with Sam getting injured over it, his guilt was compounded. The fact that his son had gone out there and seen something was confirmation to him that what he saw the night Milo disappeared was not a dream. It was a nightmare, and now it almost killed his boy.

Tommy knew better than to tell his mom. It wasn't because he expected her to ground him, it was because he knew it was pointless to tell any adult. Who would believe a couple kids who said they went into the woods and found a stone structure that housed an unseen monstrosity with claws? It sounded ridiculous, like some made-up bullshit you read about in those tabloid papers while you wait in line to pay for your groceries.

But it happened. They both knew it.

And so did Tommy's friends when he told them.

"I don't doubt it," said Jerry, sucking on a lollipop outside of Sal's Market. "I always knew there was something up with our neighborhood. Between Ms. Crofton, Old Man Rooney and that creep Mr. Sadly, it's like a Halloween show."

Plop! The lollipop came out of Jerry's mouth.

Eric, Jerry and Justin laughed, but Tommy didn't. He was lost in a maze of thought, not unlike the labyrinth of woods behind Sam's house.

The rocks falling.

The darkness.

The shape of something.

"Hey, let's go check it out," said Eric.

"Check it out?" asked Jerry.

Plop! But slower and softer this time.

"You aren't scared, are you, Jerry?"

Jerry shoved the lollipop back in his mouth, hardening his look and crossing his arms.

"Do I look scared to you?" he muffled out. "Who knows? Maybe whatever is down there has something to do with all these other pets disappearing, too. Maybe this is our chance to become heroes!"

"That's not a bad idea," said Justin. "Last time Tommy went he was only with Sam. If we're there with him then there's no way this thing will get away." Jerry, Eric, and Justin looked to Tommy.

The screech.

Artie's bark.

"Tommy? Earth to Tommy," Justin said, waving his hand in front of Tommy's face.

"The sound it made ..." Tommy said, trailing off and looking beyond his friends in a daze. "Artie saved us."

"He sure did," said Eric. "That's what makes him Awesome Artie and your best friend. And we're your friends too, Tommy. So, let's go check this thing out together."

"Yeah," Tommy said, blinking back to reality. "Let's find out what's down there."

TWENTY-TWO

The sun was setting on Sunfish Lane and that meant it was time for Carl Crocker to put on his jacket that read SECURITY in large, bold letters on its back. It fit like a knife going into its sheath. Crocker loved it.

He stood in front of the full-length mirror in his darkening bedroom next to his dresser where he kept a picture of Deborah from their vacation to Italy. In the photo she was smiling brightly and wearing a black sundress punctuated with a pink floral design, her golden-blond hair cascading over her shoulders. She loved the food and views there. The plane ride? Not so much.

It was during that vacation that she started to feel ill. At first, they thought it was something she ate. Too much fine Italian cuisine, they joked.

If only.

Once they returned home, she immediately made an appointment and saw her doctor. A blood test and a screening later, she was delivered what she kiddingly referred to as her "final notice."

That trip to Italy seemed like a lifetime ago to Crocker, a dream he wished he never woke up from.

He stared into the mirror, buttoned the last button on his

jacket—always starting from the bottom and finishing at the top —and grinned.

"Good evening, what brings you out tonight?" he said to his reflection.

The day's waning orange light cut across his big toothy smile in thin lines from between the nearby window's blinds. He dropped the smile and cleared his throat; a piece of his hair had fallen out of place. He pushed it back with his hand and tried again.

"Well, hello there. What brings you out this fine evening?" Better, but not perfect.

He reached over to his bed and picked up a long and black cylindrical object encased in a black leather protector. He took it out and hit its other end in the palm of his hand. It was a police-issued baton meant to beat the living shit out of anyone—or anything—not willing to cooperate.

He straightened his posture and stood back in front of the mirror, now equipped with his smile and little helper.

"Howdy, neighbor. Nice night for a walk," he said, hitting the baton in his hand again. He let out a deep, obnoxious laugh.

Better. Much better.

Twenty-Three

The quickest way back to the clearing in the woods was through Sam's backyard. Given that he was on lockdown with his mother keeping an eagle eye on any activity happening around their house, Tommy and the others couldn't chance it. Tommy decided instead to set the meeting spot just below Old Man Rooney's house. The hill he lived on top of was at the other end of the street near the cul-de-sac and at the bottom of the hill was another entrance to the woods. It would take longer to get there, but at least this way they wouldn't be seen.

Sneaking out of the house was the easy part for Tommy because his mother Beth worked the night shift as a nurse at Brighton Falls Nursing and Retirement Home, making just enough money to keep a modest roof over their heads. The 8 P.M. curfew set by Crocker made things trickier, however, and Tommy felt like he was under a microscope as he waited for his friends on the deserted street.

He checked his watch: 7:47 P.M.

Melancholic dusk faded into night as darkness settled in. Tommy sat on his bike on the edge of the road next to the trees and near a telephone pole. A piece of paper was stapled to it with a picture of Milo framed in a box that said MISSING in red letters. The black Lab looked longingly out of the small box it was trapped inside of on the pole.

Two more sheets of paper were stapled to the telephone pole, one above and one below Milo. The one on top was of Cooper, the Stevens's bulldog, and the one below was Zazzie, the Jones's black-haired cat. Both had gone missing two days apart earlier in the week. The latest additions to a growing number of missing pets in the area.

Tommy waited for his friends, hoping they would soon show.

They weren't the only ones out tonight. The summertime crickets chirped their constant song, with embellishments added in by invisible tree frogs. Tommy had never actually seen a tree frog before. But judging by how loud they were, it was impossible not to believe they were real. The combination of the two made for a comforting sound that reassured you the world was alive and well, at least for the time being.

Artie was safe and sound at home. No way was Tommy going to bring him back out to the woods, not after last time. He gave the pup his dinner and medicine before he left and brought him outside in the yard to take care of his business. Like always, Artie didn't want to go back inside. He loved the summer song of the crickets and tree frogs. He would stay out there all night if he could, listening intently and occasionally lifting his head up, nose pointed toward the sky, to catch the refreshing night breeze. He always snuck a peek at Tommy when he did this, as if to check and see if he was enjoying it, too. Tommy did, and on that night, he did a little bit more.

Tommy had placed his friend on the couch and gave him a hug before leaving.

"I'm going back out there to find out what that was," he said to Artie.

Artie looked at him, listening.

Tommy took a blanket and wrapped it around the thinning dog. His ribs were beginning to show and half of his dinner still sat in his bowl. Getting him to eat was becoming harder and harder.

"You just get some rest and I'll be back as soon as I can."

Tommy opened the door, looked back at Artie, gave him a wink, and left. Artie watched him as he went out the door.

Now, in the vacant night, Artie weighed heavily on Tommy's mind as he waited alone for his friends. He felt like he was about to cry and stopped himself.

Someone was approaching.

A tall shadow swayed back and forth under the moonlight down the quiet street, making its way to Tommy. Tommy clenched the handles on his bike hard, ready to jet to avoid being spotted.

"Nice night, isn't it?" the voice asked.

Tommy couldn't make out who it was. It sounded as though the person was eating.

"You're getting crumbs on me, quit it," said a second voice. "How am I the fat one and you're the one who's always eating?"

The swaying shadow finally made its way close enough to Tommy for him to tell who it was: Jerry and Eric. Eric was pedaling his bike and Jerry was sitting on top of the handlebars.

The balancing act came to a stop and Jerry hopped off.

"Nice night," Jerry continued, with a cookie in his hand, "... to kill a monster." He walked behind Eric and pulled out two aluminum baseball bats from a backpack attached to the bike, the same ones they used when playing down at the ballfield.

"Where's Justin?" asked Tommy.

"Ask and you shall receive!" a voice blurted out from behind him. Tommy jumped and turned around. Justin was gliding up behind him on his bike.

"Keep it down," said Tommy.

"Yeah, we don't want to ruin the element of surprise for the boogeyman," Jerry said with a smirk.

"You guys don't get it," said Tommy. "But you will. There's something back there in those woods."

"Trees. Lots and lots of trees," said Justin.

Jerry laughed and took another bite out of his cookie. It was chocolate chip, judging by all the chocolate around his mouth.

"Hey, don't forget this is our big chance to get on the front page of the *Brighton Falls Gazette*," Jerry said. He waved his hand across the air, reading a fake headline only he could see.

"Jerry Redman and friends slay pet killer, Redman and Sarah Lackey wed."

"Give it up, man," Eric said, trying not to laugh.

Ignoring this, Justin turned his attention to Tommy. "And what are we going to do if we see this thing?" he asked.

"Swing away," Tommy said, taking out his own bat and holding it up.

Twenty-Four

Carl Crocker swung the door to his red Buick shut as he stepped out to begin his nightly patrol. He parked it off to the side of the road near the entrance to Sunfish Lane in a twilight zone where a bed of daisies grew and no one laid claim to the property. He was safe putting it there without anyone complaining, he figured. Not that anyone would complain to their good neighbor Mr. Crocker, anyway. The way the residents of Sunfish Lane saw it, they all owed him a huge debt of gratitude for his decision to provide a watch and protect them.

Judy Simmons had decided to show her appreciation with a homemade meatloaf that she dropped off to him earlier in the week. He had thanked her kindly and waved goodbye to her after she handed him the warm Tupperware container, but she lingered—as she usually did when around Crocker—before eventually catching her cue to leave like someone who just remembered they left the oven on.

Crocker packed some of that meatloaf with him tonight and left it on the passenger's seat of his car. It was terrible. Godawful. But on the off chance that busybody Judy Simmons decided to pop up on him, he planned on telling her how much he loved it by showing her he had it with him.

And that's how you keep them eating out of your hand, he thought to himself.

There wasn't really any competition for his unofficial spot as the neighborhood's guardian, although Crocker could smell the growing stench of jealousy from George Farrison becoming stronger and stronger in recent weeks. Crocker had started to take great pride in his duties, and he wasn't about to let anyone come along and make a fool of him. Farrison had the experience thanks to his time watching over the docks down at the ferry boat, making him the only one around with a fighter's chance of taking Crocker's place. Crocker knew that Farrison was in fact the one with the more qualified credentials, but he'd never admit it. The old Crocker charm allowed him to snatch up what he wanted yet again.

Crocker strolled down the street, whistling Johnny Cash's "Ring of Fire." It was his wife's favorite and she used to sing it all the time. She's the one who introduced him to the Man in Black and expanded his music palette, a palette that was nonexistent before he met her. He kept her records and would listen to them at night, lost in thought.

The headlights of an old pickup truck approaching from a bend up ahead flashed around the corner, momentarily lighting up the darkening neighborhood before its driver clicked them down to parking lights to supposedly not blind Crocker. The only light Crocker was using to guide his way was the moon and the lantern lights in the front yards of the houses he walked by.

Every house had one, and they created a faint yellow glow along the edge of the black street, like the Yellow Brick Road fading away.

The pickup truck slowed down and came to a stop next to Crocker.

"Good evening, sir," the voice inside the truck said.

Crocker cringed when he turned and saw who rolled up beside him. Lo and behold it was George Farrison, retired ferry boat security guard and wannabe hero. Farrison, big and burly, was pouring out of the small pickup truck. His arm hung out of the window and he gave a wave.

"Well, howdy, neighbor," Crocker said and smiled, waving back and trying not to choke on his words.

"Nice night for a walk, no?" Farrison asked.

By the looks of it you could use a good walk, Crocker thought to himself.

Crocker's grin widened. "Sure is. Couldn't ask for a nicer one."

"You let me know if you find that creep who's been killing those pets," Farrison said, without returning the smile. "I got something for him."

"I have it all handled here, Mr. Farrison. Thanks for your offer. You have a safe night now."

"You just let me know," replied Farrison, not breaking the stern expression on his face.

He clicked his headlights back on and drove off, likely heading to an AA meeting, Crocker surmised.

Crocker dropped his smile and quickened his pace.

TWENTY-FIVE

Y ou know, I kinda missed this," Jerry said, twirling his bat around.

"Missed what?" asked Justin.

Jerry, Eric and Justin were making their way through the woods with Tommy leading the pack. The moon was full and the light from it provided a natural spotlight on the inky outlines of the trees that stood in their way. If not for the moon, they wouldn't be able to see where they were going. In the dim glow coming from the giant hanging sphere above them, the forest seemed to go on forever and ever, the arches in the tree limbs creating shadowed smiles laughing and mocking them for their effort.

"Getting lost in the wood with you guys," answered Jerry.

"We're not lost," Tommy said. "I know where we're going."

Then, to himself: *Where is this place? We should be there by now.*

Tommy was really beginning to feel like they were lost, like those trees really were laughing at them, laughing at *him* for daring to come back. They might even start talking. Who knows what happens out here after dark? Maybe this was a mistake.

Maybe he's getting all of his friends into something they don't deserve.

"If you know where we're going then why haven't we found it yet? We've been out here for almost a half hour. And why did that trail just disappear?" Jerry said back. "And you know what else? We all must be really stupid because no one here even bothered to bring a flashlight! We're just a bunch of stupid kids, aren't we?"

"Jesus, Jerry. Don't you ever shut up?" Eric said.

"I'm just saying, we've been walking and walking and still haven't come across any blood-hungry demons," Jerry said. "This isn't like the movies at all."

"Any movie with you in it would be a dud anyway," Eric laughed.

"You'd pay to see it," Jerry said. "You'd even buy it on—"

Tommy came to a quick stop, catching the others by surprise and causing Jerry to run into his back.

"There it is," Tommy said, a weight of relief coming out with the words. "We're here."

"Where's here?" asked Justin. "I don't see anything."

Tommy carefully stepped forward, pushing tree branches out of his way. His friends followed.

Before them was the clearing, and in its center stood the mangled edifice with rocks still scattered across the ground from when Tommy and Sam were there before. The vines and roots snarled around it made Eric think it was something meant to be left alone. Certainly not something meant for a group of kids to mess with.

"That's it?" Jerry quipped. "Looks like just a pile of shitty rocks."

"You said something in there tried to get you, Tommy?" asked Eric.

"Something. Whatever it was it had sharp claws and made an awful screeching sound," said Tommy.

"You sure it wasn't just a raccoon?" Justin asked. "Or a fisher cat? Those things can make weird noises."

"A what cat? I've never heard of a raccoon actually grabbing someone and pulling them," Tommy said, a little annoyed. "Or leaving orange ooze behind."

Jerry cleared his throat. "Guys, I hate to say it. I think our buddy Tommy has been spending too much time watching those crappy horror movies on Netflix."

"Don't lie, you love those," Eric said. This was a universal truth. Jerry was addicted to streaming horror movies and would stay up late at night watching them alone, trying to scare himself.

Jerry brushed off Eric's comment, bumped past Tommy and strolled toward the rock structure with the swagger of a kid who just had his first kiss. He twirled his bat some more.

"Tommy, if you want to watch a good scary movie, you have to expand your horizon," he said. "Everyone knows that no good horror story would ever center around a lame pile of rocks."

Jerry kicked a couple of the loose rocks. He bent down and picked one up. "And as far as whatever's down there is concerned," he said, leaning back and ready to throw the rock down the hole, "it's probably just your everyday rabid squirrel."

With a lazy turn of his arm, Jerry flung the rock into the structure's round opening and watched it disappear into the emptiness within it.

Click. Clack. Click.

They listened as the rock made its way down the hole, ricocheting off the sides and sounding farther and farther away. They waited to hear it land at the bottom but were met with silence. A second ticked by and Jerry, still holding his follow-through stance, looked over at his friends.

"Did you feel that?" he asked them.

"Stop it with the jokes, Jerry," Justin said, not amused.

"Feel what?" Tommy asked, then threw his arms up in the air, trying to keep his balance.

The ground quivered with two massive shakes in rapid succession. Jerry held onto his glasses so they wouldn't fall off. Neither Tommy nor his friends were ready for the noise that followed.

They all covered their ears immediately. At first, Tommy thought it sounded like screeching car brakes. It made him think of the time when he was driving with his mom in her old beat-up car and they almost got in an accident because the brakes were giving out. But the low, gurgling, guttural sound that followed had to be filled with so much dirt and earth that it couldn't be machine.

It was alive and it was angry.

"What the hell is in there?!" Justin yelled.

Jerry dropped his bat. He stared in shock at the pile of shitty rocks. No doubt about it, this wasn't any type of raccoon or rabid squirrel.

Tommy grabbed Jerry by his shirt. "Now do you believe me?"

"What is it?" Jerry asked, a shake in his voice.

Jerry pulled himself away from Tommy and leaned himself over the edge of the stone structure's opening, adjusting his glasses and looking down into it, trying to catch a glimpse of whatever lay below.

"Jerry, I wouldn't—"

"Hey, who's out there?" a voice called out from somewhere behind them.

"T-Tommy ..." Jerry stuttered.

Tommy turned to see where the voice was coming from and saw a flashlight close in the distance. Then he turned his attention back to Jerry.

"Tommy," Jerry continued. "I-I want to go home."

Jerry looked at Tommy with the scared and confused expression of a helpless baby as he collapsed on his bottom and began to rock back and forth. He was trembling and had wet himself. Tommy noticed his face had become as pale as the moon, his eyes stuck in a stare.

"I saw it," Jerry said. "I want to go home."

"You saw it? What is it?"

"I just want to go home. Can we go home now?"

"Yes, but tell me first what you saw in there."

Jerry seemed to have lost his normally colorful vocabulary and just kept repeating over and over in a voice that was not quite his own: *I want to go home. I want to go home.*

"What's wrong with him?" Eric blurted out, his own voice breaking.

"Hey! I said who's out there!" the bodiless voice said again, this time with obvious anger.

There was someone else in the woods coming their way and Tommy could feel a string of panic beginning to wrap tightly around him and his friends.

"I don't know," Tommy said, trying to get Jerry up off the ground. "He's dead weight." Eric and Justin rushed over and helped Tommy pick Jerry up.

"Snap out of it, Jerry! This isn't time for your jokes!" Justin said.

Jerry didn't blink. He just kept saying *I want to go home.*

"Oh my God, what's wrong with you?" Eric said. There was no masking the sound of fright in Eric's voice. He was on the edge of tears seeing his friend in such a vulnerable state.

"We have to get out of here," said Justin. "We can't let whoever that is see us."

"Maybe they can help?" asked Eric.

"You're going to trust a stranger in the woods in the middle of night?"

"He's right," Tommy said to Eric. "Let's go back into the woods on the other side of the opening and see who it is first, and then maybe they can help us."

Tommy and Justin each took one of Jerry's arms and slung it around their neck. They carried him back into the woods on the far side of the clearing, out of view and opposite the direction the stranger was approaching. Eric tagged behind, looking over his shoulder.

Justin paused for a moment, trying to regain his grip on Jerry's slipping arm. Jerry was heavier than his thin frame showed, Justin thought. "Man, Jeer, you gotta lay off the cookies."

Jerry didn't give a coherent reply, no zinger in return like he'd normally deliver. He just kept mumbling that he wanted to go home.

They managed to get through the thick brush and behind a wall of tree limbs to disappear from sight. Tommy and Justin slowly put Jerry back down in an upright sitting position and leaned his back up against a tree stump. He sat with a crunch, snapping twigs under himself, and continued to stare off into space.

"Get down, get down," Justin whispered.

On the other side of the clearing, the flashlight that had been moving quickly toward them came to a stop. Its handler beamed it in an arcing motion from the boys' right to left, like a lighthouse in the middle of a stormy night trying to aid a lost sailor home.

"Who's there?" the person called out. It was a man's voice, but the boys didn't recognize it.

The flashlight clicked off and the man's silhouette slipped out from the smear of trees and into the clearing.

"Who is it?" Eric whispered.

"I can't tell," Tommy said. "It might be ..."

The man walked up to the edge of the hole in the center of the clearing. He saw the stones scattered around and Jerry's baseball bat on the ground. He briefly paused again, scanning the area. He waited another moment and then continued with his business, clearly knowing exactly what he came there to do.

Below the saturating glow of the full moon, Tommy and his friends could see the shape of the man pull a rope out from a bag he was carrying. He unfurled it and let it descend into the pit.

Justin leaned forward. "Is he going down there?"

The man with the rope held his end in his hand and walked over to a nearby tree at the edge of the clearing and tied the rope around it. He made a knot and tugged it to make sure it was secure before making his way back to the stone structure in the clearing's center.

"This guy is out of his mind," said Eric.

Crazy or not, he didn't look afraid by the way he carried himself. One might even say he looked excited, like he had a hop in his step.

The man squatted down and peered over the edge into the hole surrounded by stones.

"Good morning, baby," he said. "You behaving yourself today?" The rope pulled with a tug in response.

"That's it. Jerry is right. We need to get the hell out of here," Eric said, starting to shuffle away.

"No, wait," Tommy said. "Don't you want to find out what he's doing? What's down there?"

"Yes, and I also want to live long enough to make it to high school."

"Let's just wait one more minute and then we can go, okay?" Justin said, suddenly wanting to stick around. For all of his dry, rational reasoning, Justin did enjoy flirting with danger on occasion. Plus, nothing exciting ever happened in Brighton Falls anyway, and this could be something.

Eric plumped himself halfway back in his spot. "Fine."

The three boys peered through the web of tree limbs, watching the silhouetted man conjure up what lay in the ground. There was a loud thud, quickly followed by another and that familiar feeling of the ground quivering.

For a second, Tommy thought the mystery man was going to fall in and they were never going to find out who he was or what was down there. Later, he wished that was the case.

The rope began thrashing up and down.

"There you go," said the man, coaxing the thing in the pit. "Just a little farther. I'm right here. I have a treat for you."

The man reached back into his bag and took out a small rolled up clump of something furry.

"Do you see that?" Tommy said. "Is that a ... dead animal he has in his hand?"

Another thud shook the ground and Tommy saw the man

drop the furry thing and rush to grab the rope to balance himself. That time he did almost fall in.

"There you are," he said.

Slowly, something appeared from the pit. Tommy's eyes widened.

At first it looked like a disembodied black clump, slinking up like a giant caterpillar. The round, crawling thing narrowed as more of it got closer to the top and began to take shape.

Another undefined shape came up and clutched the edge of the stone structure. Tommy realized it was a hand; a mangled and disfigured one composed of dirt with twigs jettisoning out of it. It was far larger than any normal sized hand.

The man fell on his back as the thing from the pit rose above him.

Tommy, Eric, and Justin sat and watched in awe. The thing that crept from the hole had the outline of a person, but, like its hands, the rest of its body was disproportionate and uneven. It was tall, maybe eight feet.

There were things falling from it as though it was barely staying held together, things that were alive: worms, beetles and maggots. That familiar orange liquid glop dripped down in the spaces between them.

"Ah, look at how fast you're growing," the man said, still on his back and looking up at this monstrosity with the same awe as Tommy and his friends. "And behaving so well tonight. I'm happy to be finding you where you belong."

The creature lumbered closer to the man and let out a screech.

"It's okay," the mystery man said. "What's wrong?"

It screeched again, louder and angrier, snapping Jerry out of his fog.

"Help!" Jerry shouted. He looked around startled as if he had just woken up from a deep sleep and didn't recognize where he was.

He yelled again. "Help!"

Tommy immediately lunged at him and put a hand over his

mouth to silence him, but it was too late. The man produced a long object, something that looked like a stick or cane, and used it to prop himself back up. He got to his feet and looked in the direction of Tommy and his friends.

"Time to go, guys!" said Eric, hightailing it deeper into the woods. In a second, he was gone and out of sight, no longer concerned with asking the stranger for help.

"Listen to me, Jerry," Tommy said, ignoring Eric's cowardice. Jerry stared at him with that same shocked look he had before. "You need to keep quiet."

"I-I can't—" Jerry put a hand to his chest. "I can't breathe." He started panting and grabbed Tommy's hand.

"Just hang on. Justin and I are going to get you out of here."

Justin and Tommy each took one of Jerry's arms and lifted him back up.

"Dammit! I said who's over there?" yelled the man, sounding ready to kick someone's ass.

"Shit!" Justin said. "Go! Go!"

With Jerry strapped around their shoulders, the three boys took off the same way Eric went, as fast as two people carrying a third person can.

"Do you know if this way leads back to the road?" asked Justin as they broke through tree limbs with one snap after another, swinging their baseball bats with their free hands the same way safarists do with machetes when clearing a path in a jungle. One hanging branch scratched Tommy across his forehead and he could feel the hot sting of broken skin.

"I don't know," Tommy answered. "What I do know is that we need to find help for Jerry as soon as we can, and it's definitely not coming from that guy back there."

Up ahead stood Eric, frantically looking from side to side. Tommy, Justin, and Jerry caught up to him.

"We're lost," Eric said, whipping his head back and forth.

"Well, we wouldn't be lost if you didn't chicken out and run away in the wrong direction," Justin said.

"Maybe if you guys hadn't dillydallied and left at the same time I did we wouldn't be in this situation," Eric shot back.

Justin let go of Jerry, who, despite the situation, comically sagged down. Justin stepped up close to Eric, clutching his bat by his side. The two of them had never actually fought before but it was no secret they could easily get on each other's nerves. A confrontation between the two of them had been brewing for a while. One time, in Mrs. Kretchen's science class, Eric asked Justin if he could see his paper during the middle of a test, to which Justin obliged. When Mrs. Kretchen later asked who copied who, Eric wouldn't fess up and they both failed and got detention. Justin, on the other hand, once borrowed Eric's beloved, pristine Batman comic book collection and returned it to him as a damp clump of pages after spilling soda all over it.

Accidents happen, but Justin didn't seem very sympathetic about it.

"Aren't you the one who wanted to ask that weirdo in the woods for help in the first place? I'm the one who stopped you from doing that. You should be thanking me," Justin said.

Jerry started coughing and gasping again. Tommy laid him down on the ground and held his head up with his hand.

"Guys, can you save it for later?" Tommy said. "I think he's having an asthma attack."

Justin quit his stare down with Eric and Eric begrudgingly did the same. They all knew of Jerry's trips to the nurse's office for what he called "breathing problems," but those trips always seemed to happen when it was time to take a test so none of them ever really believed him.

"Slow, deep breaths," said Tommy, trying to calm Jerry down. He had broken into a cold sweat and was shaking again.

"What do we do?" asked Eric.

"You call for help," said a voice from behind them.

The boys turned around. Standing in the moonlight above them was Carl Crocker.

"Mr. Crocker? What are you doing out here?" asked Eric.

"Wait! Back up!" Justin yelled, holding up his bat. "It was you out there."

Tommy and Eric each reached for their bat. It had to be him, right? Who else could it have been?

"Yes, I'm everywhere," said Crocker. "I'm the neighborhood watch. Didn't your parents tell you?"

Eric leaned his bat back. "You can watch me swing this bat up your—"

"Eric, wait. Maybe he can help," said Tommy. He eyed Crocker for a moment. Was it strange that Crocker was out in the woods the same time as them? Absolutely. But Jerry was in a bad way and they were in the middle of nowhere. "I think our friend is having an asthma attack or something."

"Unfortunately I don't carry an inhaler around with me. I do have these though," Crocker said. He pulled out an orange bottle of pills from his pocket. "It's anxiety medication, very low dosage. If I break one in half it should help calm him down and maybe allow him to get his breathing back under control."

Crocker moved fast, taking out a Swiss Army knife and dispensing one of the small white pills out of the bottle. He placed the pill up against a nearby tree and cut it in half with a quick push.

Bending down on his knees, he took Jerry's head from Tommy.

"My back pocket, get my water bottle and give your friend some water so he can swallow the pill," Crocker said, gesturing to Tommy. "Hurry."

Tommy followed his directions and took the bottle, placed its mouthpiece into Jerry's mouth and squeezed. Jerry coughed a little at first, taking in a small gulp of water. Crocker placed the pill in Jerry's mouth and Jerry took another gulp of water, swallowing the pill.

"Look at me, son," he said to Jerry, taking Jerry's hand and placing it on his chest. "Copy my breathing."

Crocker took long, slow breaths while holding the child's hand.

After a couple of minutes, Jerry's panicked gasps of breath slowed down and his breathing began to even back out.

"You boys aren't supposed to be out here," said Crocker in a flat voice, turning his look to the three boys standing around him. "It's past curfew."

"We were just on our way back home," said Justin.

"Me too," Crocker said. "Let's walk together."

Crocker carefully lifted Jerry back up and Tommy helped by getting Jerry on the other side. Jerry was still weak and unable to walk on his own, but he was finally calm and breathing normally again.

"You know, this is the time when things go bump in the night," Crocker said to them.

Tommy looked at his friends, all wanting to go home and out of the damn woods. "We know."

TWENTY-SIX

The neighborhood hailed Crocker as a hero for saving Jerry. The savior of Sunfish Lane had been at the right place at the right time, taking care of his duty and obligation as the neighborhood watch. Of course, Tommy and his friends were still skeptical.

They were also grounded.

Jerry's mother nearly had a heart attack the night Crocker showed up at her front doorstep with her son drugged up on anxiety medication. After she calmed down, she agreed he did what he had to do. Jerry was immediately taken to the emergency room at Brighton Falls Hospital and checked out okay, with a new inhaler in tow just in case he ever had another panic attack causing his asthma to kick in. His mother, however, decided he wouldn't be allowed to leave the house and go on any more adventures with his friends.

Crocker made it clear to all the boys' parents that it was far too dangerous for them to be out and about with the guilty party of the neighborhood's recent violent incidents still at large. The parents agreed and implemented their own strict rules regarding if and when the boys could leave their houses.

Tommy's mother's reaction was less harsh. She told Tommy

that he should know better and to stay out of the woods because "there's nothing good waiting for you out there."

Tommy, despite his initial instinct to not say anything to his mother following his time out in the woods with Sam, felt like he had to try telling her what he saw now that he truly believed it had something to do with the pets in their neighborhood disappearing.

"But you need to listen to me, Mom," he told her. "We saw someone out there carrying around a dead animal! Don't you think that might have something to do with all the missing pets and Ms. Crofton's dead cat?"

"You also claim to have seen something the size of Bigfoot," she said back to him. "I think your eyes are playing tricks on you, honey."

Tommy, to his credit, tried talking his friends into doing something about what they saw in the woods. None of them wanted any more to do with it. Justin echoed Beth's sentiment and said they just scared themselves into seeing something that wasn't actually there, while Eric admitted what he saw but was too afraid to go back. Jerry wanted to simply pretend nothing ever happened.

"I love your imagination, Tommy. Talk about some straight-to-video garbage," Jerry had said when Tommy came over to see how he was doing and to persuade Jerry to go back out to the woods with him. "Why are you so obsessed with what's out there?"

Tommy couldn't explain to Jerry why he felt the urgent need to go back there again, other than the vague possibility that it was linked to Sunfish Lane and Brighton Falls' dwindling pet population. He knew he was asking a lot, especially of Jerry, to go back. He knew that whatever was going on out there was dangerous and not going to go away on its own. It was a secret that needed to be exposed, and it was up to them to do it. If they didn't, something terrible was going to happen. It was a gut feeling.

"Listen, I'm sorry about what happened to you out there. I

really am. It's just, I can't go back there alone," Tommy said. Then, trying to entice him: "What happened to wanting to be a hero on the front page of the *Gazette*?"

"No, you listen to me, Tommy. Cut it out. Get out of my room and don't bother me anymore. I'm done hanging out with you," Jerry said, bullying Tommy toward the door of his toy-filled room. It was a mess in there—worse than Tommy's room—especially now that Jerry was spending all of his time in it instead of outside. He had become a hermit after that night in the woods, spending all day keeping to himself and playing video games.

"I don't care what you do," Jerry said to Tommy. "Go back if you want. Whatever. It makes no difference to me."

Jerry later told his mother that going into the woods was all Tommy's idea. She then did what she believed was the justified thing to do and notified Eric and Justin's parents, who upon hearing it was all Tommy's fault told their sons that they were no longer going to be spending any more time around "that boy."

Crocker caught wind of this and decided to pay a visit to Tommy's house the following week. Tommy's mother was pleased that the knocking at the door came from Mr. Crocker. The same couldn't be said for Tommy.

"Oh, Mr. Crocker," she said. "What a nice surprise. How are you?"

"I'm fine, ma'am," he smiled at her. "Thank you very much. How are you?"

Artie answered for her with a bark. He was resting in his spot on the couch before finding the strength to let the visitor know he was not unnoticed. He gingerly jumped off the couch, front paws first with a brief pause before the back two followed.

"I haven't heard him make a sound all day," said Beth.

"Is he not doing well?" asked Crocker.

"Artie's been having a hard time lately."

"Artie? I like that name."

Crocker bent down to pet the approaching dog. Artie was about to let him until something clicked once Crocker's hand got close to him. Artie instead backed away and growled at the friendly neighbor.

"Artie!" Beth said, surprised at the sick dog's response.

"He doesn't sound too sick to me," Crocker said, laughing and showing off his big pearly whites.

"I'm sorry. He usually doesn't do that."

"No worries, I won't be long anyway. I was just wondering if I could have a word with—ah, there he is."

Tommy stepped into the house from the back door. He had been in the backyard trying to set up Artie's trolley so the dog could sit around outside and enjoy the warm summer sun. Artie hustled over to Tommy's side with more than a hint of concern.

"It's okay, Art," he said.

"It sure is, Artie," said Crocker, as if he had known the dog all his life. "I'm just going to borrow your friend for a minute. Is that okay with you?"

Artie gave him a disapproving glare, the kind dogs usually reserve for when they're told not to beg for food at the dinner table.

Tommy was half expecting this. With Jerry opening his big mouth, it was only a matter of time before Crocker came calling.

"Tom, can you step outside with me for a minute?"

"Is everything all right?" asked Beth. She had a stressed look on her face that Tommy hadn't seen in a very long time.

"Oh yes. Just want to clear the air with your son."

"It's fine, mom," said Tommy.

Tommy gave Artie a pat on his head. "Be right back."

"Yes, he will," said Crocker to the dog. He looked at the beagle and winked. "See you around, Artie."

TWENTY-SEVEN

Crocker held the door open for Tommy and shut it behind him once he stepped outside.

"Let's take a seat," he told the boy.

They both sat down on the front doorstep, first Crocker then Tommy. A passerby might've guessed it was a father having a father-son talk with his child, sharing some hard-earned wisdom. Tommy never had any of those talks growing up. He knew better and he never let his guard down. That came from his own hard-earned wisdom.

"Tommy, are you okay?"

Tommy, without missing a beat, said, "Of course. Why wouldn't I be?"

Crocker clasped his hands together and leaned forward on his knees, looking out to the street as if searching for something. The waves of heat lifted from the paved road like unboxed ghosts. It wasn't the dog days of the season yet, but it was already heating up like it. Crocker, however, was wearing heavy khaki shorts and an equally uncomfortable-looking (and ugly) mustard yellow polo to complete the look. His army green dress socks traveled halfway up his calves.

"Well, I heard through the grapevine that you think you saw

something unusual out there in the woods that night I found you and your friends," Crocker said.

Tommy squinted, focusing on the footprints Crocker had left in the mulch in his mother's flower garden where he had cut across to get to the front door.

"Yeah, I did see something," Tommy said. "It turned out to only be a fisher cat. It gave me a good scare before it ran off. Never saw one in person before."

With his eyes locked on Tommy, Crocker put a hand on the boy's right shoulder. Tommy held back the urge to push it off.

"Are you sure you didn't see anything else? Because if you did then I really need to know," he said. "I haven't been able to get any leads on who killed Ms. Crofton's cat and the whereabouts of Milo. The Jones's cat is still missing and Cooper, the Stevens's bulldog is ... the list just keeps growing and it's heartbreaking. I could really use your help."

Tommy felt Crocker's hand squeeze his shoulder. "I wouldn't want anything to happen to your little buddy in there. I know what it's like to lose a pet." Tommy, wanting to pull away, kept his composure.

"If I see something, I'll let you know," he said, trying to be as casual as he could.

"And just what were you guys doing out there that night, anyway?" Crocker asked, not letting go of Tommy's shoulder.

"We were ..." Tommy's words hung in the air for a moment before Crocker snatched them.

"Just being kids. It's fine, you don't have to explain to me."

The squeeze on Tommy's shoulder lightened and the look of distress on Crocker's face eased into that patented smile he always flashed. He gave Tommy a pat on the back and got up.

"Don't worry about your pooch," he said. "I hope I didn't startle you."

"What do you mean you don't have any leads?" Tommy asked.

"I lied," Crocker said, with a small chuckle as he began to get back up and wiped the back of his shorts off. "There is one."

"Who?" Tommy asked, still sitting down.

"I shouldn't tell you this but maybe having a young fellow like yourself in the know wouldn't hurt," Crocker said. "Mr. Rooney."

"Old Ma—" Tommy started then stopped, remembering only he and his friends called the hermit on the hill Old Man Rooney, at least as far as he knew. "Mr. Rooney? Why?"

"Nothing you should have to worry your young mind about, son," Crocker said, almost feeling like he was in fact having a talk with the son he never had. "Just ... if you see anything out of the ordinary, especially with him, don't be afraid to give me a holler. Okay?"

"Okay," Tommy replied, not quite sure what Crocker meant but agreeing anyway to get rid of him faster. Tommy didn't like this guy hanging around his house. He was an uninvited guest and uninvited guests are the worst, especially ones with an arrogance like Crocker's.

Crocker smiled again and stepped down, heading toward the street. This time he followed the pebble path leading from the house to the driveway rather than taking his self-made shortcut through the flower garden.

He turned around and waved at Tommy.

Tommy watched him as he disappeared down the road, turning the corner back home and surrounded by the unboxed ghosts still rising from their paved coffins. Tommy wanted to know the truth about what was happening on his street and now he felt like he *needed* to know.

TWENTY-EIGHT

That night Tommy lay in bed, unable to sleep as he tossed and turned with Artie by his side. He was thinking about what Crocker had said to him. He didn't trust Crocker; being in the woods that night to help them seemed like too much of a coincidence. But what if there was a thread of truth to what he said?

Tommy traced his hand along the top of Artie's neck. The little guy was sleeping and tucked up into a ball against Tommy. And, from the sound of it, having himself a dream. His breathing would become heavy and then soften, and sometimes he would quickly stretch one of his legs out, inadvertently kicking Tommy, which was worth a laugh, although it usually made Tommy jump.

If there was a thread of truth to what Crocker said—if Old Man Rooney was somehow responsible for the weirdness that was happening in their neighborhood and in Brighton Falls—Tommy decided he would follow it. What he found out changed everything.

TWENTY-NINE

The heat steamed during the day but the nights could still be somewhat brisk. Such was the way for a Brighton Falls summer. That cold nip and damp air would linger through the early morning when Tommy began his paper route and would be completely gone by 10 A.M. Shorts were still always on the schedule despite the cooler mornings and Tommy planned on wearing them until late October, much to the dismay of his mother.

The next morning after Crocker's visit, she had a word to say to Tommy about his attire when he headed out the door. He nodded, telling her not to worry because it was going to be as muggy as a mutt, according to the weather guy on TV.

Tommy didn't know how to tell if it was a mutt-level of mugginess, but he was sure working up a sweat now as he whipped another paper from his satchel. It landed in the driveway to Mrs. Knox's house. She was watering her flowers and said hello. Artie, wrapped in a light blanket and sitting in the milk crate tied to the front of the bike, barked back to her in friendly recognition.

The fresh air was good for the sick dog. These rides got him out of the house without making him have to walk and strain himself. Plus, Artie loved to catch the breeze when they picked up speed.

"How are you doing up there?" Tommy asked his friend as he started to pedal faster. Artie lifted his head up and blinked his brown eyes at him as if to say *Couldn't be better! Don't slow down!*

Artie's big ears lifted in the wind like two proud flags.

Tommy had to continue pedaling fast because he was approaching the steep incline that led to Old Man Rooney's house on the hill. Not one to try and cause trouble for no good reason, Tommy had been following Rooney's request to leave the paper on his doorstep just like he asked. He hadn't seen the geezer in weeks, so he must have been doing it right. Except for the one time he came out to yell at him, Tommy had never before seen Rooney step foot out of his house.

But today had to be different. Tommy wasn't going to leave the paper where Rooney wanted it. Instead, he was going to coax the old man to come back out. Tommy had questions that he thought only Rooney could answer, for better or worse.

Tommy peddled faster, knowing he was going to get himself into possibly another confrontation with an old guy who had a temper as hot as the sun he was now pedaling under. No matter, what could Old Man Rooney possibly do to him?

Nearing the hermit's house, Tommy saw something that caused him to slam on his brakes. Artie directed his head at what Tommy was looking at.

To Tommy's surprise, he wouldn't need to spark Rooney to come out of his seclusion—the old man was already standing on his front step. Dressed in his green bathrobe and with his white frazzled hair sticking out from the sides, Rooney stood stoically like a statue emoting absolutely nothing. He had been waiting for Tommy.

He cleared his throat and pointed his cane at the boy and his dog.

"I need to talk to you about your pup," he said.

THIRTY

There was a fire Tommy could see in Old Man Rooney's eyes when he stepped closer to the hermit, a fire brighter than the sun beaming down on them that summer morning. He seemed to have a newfound purpose, a boost of energy that inspired him to, at the very least, leave the safe confines of his walls and stand on his deck under his own accord.

"What about him?" Tommy asked, putting a protective hand over Artie. Tommy could tell Artie was about to lunge toward Rooney, ignoring the fact that he was much weaker than the last time he did. Tommy didn't want that scene replaying itself.

In the front of his mind, Tommy remembered what Crocker said about Rooney. Now, however, with Rooney standing and waiting for him, he for some reason wasn't afraid. He had a strange feeling that he could trust him, and he didn't know why.

"Let's go inside and talk instead of having a staring contest out here," Rooney said, slowly changing his course of direction back to the house. "Don't need no busy bodies around here poking their noses in where they don't belong."

Tommy hesitated. Sensing this, Rooney stopped and looked back at him. "You know, this would be a lot easier if you helped me," he said, gesturing at the climb up the steps.

"Why should I follow you into your house, especially after what happened last time?" Tommy asked. "I don't even know you."

"That's right," Rooney said. "You don't know me. There's a lot you don't know that you should. And I'm going to tell you all of it. Now let's put last time behind us. You've been doing well with your paper delivery so I no longer have any qualms about you."

He glared at Tommy with his gray eyes. The thirteen-year-old boy wondered if he was being sized up for a fight.

"You love your dog?" Rooney asked him.

Artie barked, answering for both of them.

A smile spread across Rooney's hairy face, revealing gaps of missing teeth and faded dimples of a past youth.

"That's what I thought," he said. "Now let's get a move on."

THIRTY-ONE

The inside of Old Man Rooney's house was as dusty and old as Tommy expected. What he wasn't expecting were all of the fish tanks. He noticed most of them were empty except for a few, including the largest one in the living room. Brightly colored yellow and blue fish pierced through its green and murky water.

If he doesn't change the water soon, those fish are going to be in worse shape than the guy who feeds them, Tommy thought to himself.

Other than the fish tanks, there wasn't anything in Rooney's house that caught Tommy by surprise. There were lots of prescription pill bottles—a staple of an elderly person's residence, Tommy presumed—and shaggy old quilt rugs. And no, there weren't any kids' bones like Jerry had gleefully described. There were a lot of boxes overflowing with photos all over the place, reminding Tommy of a home he had seen on a TV program about people who collect too many things and can't seem to let any of them go. Out of all those pictures trying to escape from the boxes, only one was in a frame on a small table in the living room next to a well-worn chair. It was a faded photo of a young and pretty woman on the beach with the ocean behind her. Her hair style and clothes belonged to a different time, decades in the past.

"Who's this in the photo?" Tommy asked.

"My wife," Rooney said, without turning around. He said it in a matter-of-fact way like Tommy should have already known.

"I didn't know you were married."

"Yes. I was. Once, a long time ago."

"She died?"

Again, in the same matter-of-fact tone: "Yes. Car wreck."

"I'm sorry," Tommy said.

"What can you do?" Rooney said. There was a hint of real questioning in his response, not a complete off-handed quip, that stuck out to Tommy. It caught him off guard. Rooney continued shuffling around the maze of boxes and fish tanks to get to the kitchen in the back, limping with every other step. It was a wonder he could make it around everything. A few of the boxes looked crushed, Tommy noticed, and he guessed it was from Rooney losing his balance and falling on top of them.

Rooney turned the stovetop on to heat the kettle and then pulled out a chair from the cluttered table. Light snuck into the room between dirty drapes hanging in front of the window next to the table, illuminating a mess of papers, mostly bills, thrown there.

"Sit," he said to Tommy, gesturing at the chair.

Tommy held Artie in his arms, still wrapped in his blanket. The fact that he hadn't tried to dash out from Tommy's grasp and bark Old Man Rooney away from them was a sullen reminder to Tommy of just how sick his friend had become. Although weak, Artie's eyes stayed locked on the strange man. They followed his every move with fixated study.

Tommy hesitated and then sat down, looking at the mountain of unopened mail spread before him.

How does he eat here? Tommy wondered. And Tommy immediately knew the answer: he doesn't. Rooney hadn't eaten at that table in years.

"He's not well, is he?" Rooney asked, glancing over at Artie while tending to the kettle.

"He's ..." Tommy said, trying to find a way to avoid going into too much detail.

"It's okay, you can spare me all the medical mumbo jumbo. Does he have much time left?"

Tommy thought this question cold and didn't care for Rooney's casual inquiry about the remaining days of his best friend. "No, he doesn't," Tommy responded.

"Shame. But I bet you wouldn't want those days to be cut short, right?" Rooney asked. Without waiting for Tommy to answer, he added: "Tea should be ready in three minutes."

Rooney turned his back to the kettle and pulled out a seat across the table from Tommy. He sat down with a plump after taking a second to aim his landing. He let out a small *oomph* before regaining his composure, as poor and slouched as it was. Rooney stared over at Tommy and lowered his head, the way a parent would when disciplining a child.

"Crocker has been selling you a crock of shit," he said.

"What?" Tommy said, stirring in his seat. This whole situation was mighty uncomfortable. In no way did Tommy feel in danger anymore—misguided youthful confidence gave Tommy the false impression that he could fight off the old man if he needed—there was, however, this unmistakable sense that he was about to learn something he would later wish he hadn't. He realized that now there was no turning back. After all, this is what he wanted, wasn't it? To get to the bottom of what increasingly felt like growing tentacles of secrets suffocating his neighborhood? To prevent any more pets from possibly vanishing or getting hurt?

"I know all about what you and your friends have been up to," Rooney said. "Talk about busybodies!" He cackled and Artie's ears shot up. Tommy felt a sudden pit in his stomach. "Don't worry, kiddo, because I also know what that two-face crock-o'-shit Crocker has been up to, too," the old man continued, now lowering his volume back down to a respectable inside voice.

"He said something about you, too," Tommy shot back with a gleam of suspicion.

A wicked smile came across Rooney's face yet again. Tommy had seen him smile more times in the past minute than he had in his entire life leading up to this.

"Oh, I'm sure he's been saying a lot. That fella sure likes to talk. Always has," said Rooney.

Another cackle from the old man and this time Artie countered it with a bark.

"Calm down, old boy," the old man said to the dog, giving him a wave.

Like Artie, Tommy's patience was growing thin. This is what he wanted in a roundabout way—to get information from Rooney that could hopefully help him figure out exactly what happened in the woods. If Crocker had an eye on Rooney, then the recluse living in the house on the hill must know something. But Tommy wasn't expecting Artie to be brought into the conversation. It made him uneasy.

"You said you had something to tell me regarding my dog," Tommy said, becoming more annoyed.

"Yes, yes. I see the two of you and it reminds me of an old friend I used to have. Buttons was her name. A beautiful sheep dog that didn't have a mean bone in her body. You want to know what happened to her?" Rooney paused and then opened his mouth as if about to say, but stopped again and closed it. His eyes glazed over as he became lost in thought. After a moment, he snapped out of it and looked Tommy dead in the eye.

"She got gobbled up," he said. "Like a hot supper on a Friday night."

"Eaten?" Tommy asked.

"Did I stutter?" the old man countered. "Yes! Gobbled up! Gone!"

"That's terrible," Tommy said, unconsciously tightening his

hold on Artie. The dog let out a small whimper as if he also understood what Rooney had said. "Coyotes?" Tommy asked.

Rooney shook his head no and let out a little laugh as if he was expecting Tommy to ask that.

"It sure was terrible and I don't want the same thing happening to your pooch right there," Rooney said, pointing a crooked, arthritis-gnarled index finger at Artie. "These pets dying and going missing around here aren't a coincidence! The same thing happened around the time I lost my Buttons."

The old man drew in a deep breath, put both his elbows up on the table, and shot an icy look across the table at Tommy.

"That place you've been going to in those woods, it's evil."

Eeeeeee!!!

The kettle screamed a high-pitched cry, and Tommy jumped.

"A smart kid like you, I reckon you already know that and that's why you decided to follow me in here," Rooney said. "And if I were a betting man, I'd also say you don't know why it's no good or how it came to be that way."

The old man pushed himself up and did his limp-shuffle over to the kettle. He picked up a small, white porcelain cup with purple flowers painted around it and splintered spiderweb cracks to match. He dropped a cheap no-name tea bag into it and then poured the hot water from the kettle.

"Tea?" he asked Tommy.

"And what exactly does Crocker have to do with this?" Tommy asked, ignoring the offer and wanting to get to the heart of the matter.

Rooney huffed and slowly got back to his seat. "In a rush, I see."

He placed the small cup carefully down on top of a saucer dish. Tommy could see the steam rising from the cup. It blanketed Rooney's face and gave him a ghostly portrait.

"That was him you and your friends saw out there the other night at the wishing well."

"That was Crocker? At the ... wishing well?" Tommy asked.

Now that he thought about it, that shitty pile of rocks circling the hole in the ground did resemble some type of well. Maybe not something from a bright and happy fable, but something more akin to a Grimms' fairy tale.

"One of the perks, or curses, of living up here on the hill is that I can see everything that goes on down below. Even in the clearing in the woods, if the moonlight is just right. Even the godforsaken wishing well."

"It looked like just a pile of rocks and a hole in the ground to us," Tommy said.

"Yep, that's what happens when you're hundreds of years old," Rooney said, taking a sip of his tea. "Ya fall apart and look like shit."

He put his teacup back down, looking more and more by the second like a phantom behind the rising steam. "I'm going to tell you something and you're going to laugh. I hope you come to your senses for your own well-being and that of your pup."

Rooney straightened his back as best he could.

"Contrary to what you all have been led to believe, this town isn't built on a rosy and cheery foundation, and that wishing well has stayed a secret for a reason," Rooney said. "It's a gravesite, a place of death, not miracles. You ever hear of Dorsey Beckingham?"

Now Tommy was thoroughly confused. "Yes," he said. "She was hanged for going crazy and killing her three children back in the 1600s. We learned about it in our local history class." Tommy remembered because Jerry wouldn't stop talking about it. He even went to the library on his own to find out more. *The library.* Jerry hated the library.

"But did Brighton Falls 101 include the part where Dorsey was accused of being someone who dabbled in, what do you call it? The dark arts? Spooky business? When they found her children, they also found the walls in her home covered in gibberish writing. Apparently, she didn't have a pen so she used her children's blood. She said she was going to bring them back to life.

People around here believed she was a witch, so they had her executed in that very clearing where you and your little buddies ventured out," Rooney said, pointing out the dirty window with his equally dirty thumb.

"Turns out our forefathers were the suspicious type, and thorough. To make sure the so-called witch was dead for good, they chopped her up, threw her remains in the well and lit the whole thing on fire."

"Sure, whatever you say," Tommy said, not believing a word coming out of Rooney's mouth and beginning to think he was wasting his time. "I think you need to get outside more. Why do you always stay cooped up in here, anyway? You know the place my mom works at has a van that comes out and picks people like you up. You could—"

BAM! Old Man Rooney slammed his skinny little twisted fist down on the table, causing his tea to jump out of its cup and Tommy out of his seat. Artie let out a bark.

"You're not listening to me," the old man growled.

"Okay, okay, I'm listening," Tommy said, trying not to look shaken.

Again, Old Man Rooney's wicked smile showed itself. He leaned back in close to Tommy the way people do when telling a secret.

He continued, "And she wasn't the only one. Turns out she had followers, her own little witch fan club. They tried to snatch up all the town's children to stage some sort of public display of death and rebirth, trying to pick up where Dorsey left off and prove to everyone that she was right, but it wasn't long before their hocus pocus ran out and the locals caught up to them and stopped them just in time. They threw that bunch of bitches down in the well with ol' Dorsey."

Rooney stopped and took another sip of his tea. "Betcha Brighton Falls 101 didn't teach you that," he said. The old man seemed proud of himself, as if springing this yarn on Tommy relieved him of some kind of burden.

"And how do you know all this?" Tommy asked.

"Let's just say that part doesn't concern you just yet," Rooney said, stroking his white beard.

"Okay, so let me get this straight. The people that lived in Brighton Falls over three hundred years ago executed a group of witches in the woods and threw their remains in the well and lit it on fire and now it's haunted?"

"Cursed," Rooney said, correcting Tommy.

"Whatever, same thing."

"No, it's not," Rooney snapped back.

Tommy held Artie tightly. "I'm confused," he said. "What does this have to do with what's happening now? What does this have to do with my dog?"

"I'm getting to that," the old man said.

He took another sip of tea and cleared his throat.

"After these so-called witches were done away with, the next generation of townspeople began to second guess the public executions their parents performed. The well became a place of mourning for a brief time, a place where people went to leave flowers for the women killed there. Eventually the townspeople decided to have all records of the well and what happened there wiped from the history books. All's well that ends well," Rooney chuckled.

"It was only a matter of time before someone found that well, and sure enough someone did," he said. "About seventy years ago, a group of teenagers came across it and started calling it a wishing well. It became a place where local sweethearts would go to cast their dreams into the unknown with a good luck kiss in hopes that they would someday be realized, only to be eventually disappointed. Isn't love grand?"

Rooney readjusted himself in his seat. He looked suddenly uncomfortable, Tommy thought.

"Anyway, a lovestruck fool's letterman boyfriend on the swimming team dove down in a big meet and didn't come back up. She took it hard and did what any heartbroken young lady would do in that situation: go to the wishing well and wish Mr. Varsity back. The girl, however, wasn't your average pigtailed girl-next-door, oh no. This one had a dark side not much different than that group of ladies I was just telling you about. She had tasted some of Ms. Beckingham's home cooking and got hooked. Where she found the recipe, I'll never know. Probably Sherwinkle and his crappola Books and Beyond shop. He's always been known to have some questionable contacts. Anyway, she decided to use that recipe to get her crush back in what some might call a blood pact."

Rooney stopped, took another sip of his tea, and squinted. "Gone cold," he croaked.

"So, did he come back?" Tommy asked, half amused. The old man's story sounded like one of those straight-to-video movies that Jerry always hated on but secretly loved to talk about, when Sarah Lackey wasn't around, of course. Rooney sure had a convincing way of telling it, though.

"Well, in a way he did."

"What do you mean?"

"The wishing well can do whatever you ask of it if you know how to ask. But the most important thing to remember is that there is always a price to pay when it comes to using the wishing well," Rooney said, eyes locked on Tommy.

"Okay, that's enough," Tommy said. "Nice story. I can't believe you actually expect me to believe this. I thought this was going to have something to do with my dog."

Old Man Rooney shook his head, contemplating something. He pulled up on the tea bag's thin white string like someone bobbing a fishing line to see if they have a bite.

"That girl was Janice, my sister," he said. "And that thing you saw in the woods is coming for your dog next."

"I don't believe you," Tommy said with a shake in his voice. He could feel the hurt in his heart finally bubbling up and trying to escape from his throat. It was him not wanting to believe more than anything else. He felt dizzy with too much information and just wanted to forget everything he saw and everything this old crackpot just spewed at him. He wanted to go back to being a kid again, with a healthy Artie and nothing to worry about except getting his homework done.

And how could this old man—this stranger—blatantly threaten Artie?

Tommy pushed his seat back and stood up. "I'm out of here," he said.

With Artie safely in his arms, Tommy moved to the front door, not caring at all if Rooney tried to stop him. As far as Tommy was concerned, as soon as he stepped through that front door and back outside, it was back to reality and away from this loony bin.

"Haven't you noticed that your friend is the last pet left on Sunfish Lane?" Rooney asked.

Tommy hadn't noticed that, and now that Rooney pointed it out, he was right.

"This thing, it feeds, Tommy. First on small animals to gain its strength, then it works its way up to ..." Rooney said, not finishing his sentence. "I've seen it firsthand with my Buttons, and my sister. I didn't stop it in time to save them. I didn't know how. That's why I'm telling you."

Tommy placed his hand on the doorknob and stopped, his back still facing Rooney.

"The difference between curses and hauntings is curses can be broken," said the old man.

"How?" Tommy asked.

Old Man Rooney lifted himself up out of his seat and made his way over to a dust-ridden bookshelf. His bony finger traced along the spines of nondescript books and stopped on a black one. He pulled it out, a ravaged and worn book that was peeling and had no words or images on its front or back.

"I'll tell you," the old man said. "But you have to promise me something."

THIRTY-TWO

Tommy went back home that morning feeling numb. He was overwhelmed by the sense that he had gotten himself into something way over his head, something no kid belonged in the middle of.

Could Old Man Rooney be full of it? Tommy hoped he was, but again that gut feeling crept up and told him the old man wasn't.

Tommy's plan to find out more, to try and play Rooney and Crocker off of each other, had left him feeling like the one played. For years no one talked to Rooney, the hermit on the hill. Now that Tommy had spoken to him, he knew why.

And what about those things he said about Artie?

Tommy, as much as he may have laughed off what the old man said, couldn't ignore his threats.

The ailing beagle had trudged through the kitchen upon returning home with Tommy, making a stop at his food and water bowls without having a taste from either before deciding to take a nap. He circled around the center of Tommy's room and stepped up on the side of the bed with his two front paws, looking for Tommy, like he always did, for a boost up the rest of the way. Once up, Artie stretched his short legs out and rolled over on his side, sprawling out on the bed and making himself comfortable. The talk with Rooney seemed to have taken something extra out of the dog, too.

"What do you think?" Tommy asked his faithful friend.

Artie let out a yawn, peaceful and serene like all animal yawns should be.

"Thanks for the input," Tommy said, smiling, and kissed the pooch on the cheek. "Don't worry, Artie. I'm always going to be right here."

Artie blinked his soft eyes at Tommy. Tommy reached over and placed the blue blanket on the bed over half of the dog to keep him warm. It was summer and quite hot, but Artie always had a coolness to him now since losing so much weight from becoming sick. The once plump and energetic thirty-five-pound beagle had become a slower and weaker sixteen-pound shell of himself. Tommy made a habit to take Artie in once a week to Dr. Finney to get weighed. No matter how much food Tommy got him to eat, each time they went Artie would weigh less and less.

Dr. Finney told Tommy that Artie's quality of life would need to be taken into account as his condition worsened. These last couple of days that quality of life meter had fallen drastically, plummeting so much so that Tommy was afraid if he left Artie alone for even a minute, something would happen to him by the time he got back. There was nothing else they could do for Artie at this point, Dr. Finney told Tommy. Just making Artie as comfortable as possible was all he could control.

Tommy wasn't about to give up on his friend, though. That's not what friends do; two- legged friends and four-legged friends alike. And Artie had proven to be a much better friend than most of the two-legged ones Tommy knew.

THIRTY-THREE

Rum was Crocker's favorite. Add in a touch of cola—but not too much, you don't want to ruin your drink—and it was smooth sailing for the neighborhood protector. Of course, no one on Sunfish Lane would ever think of Crocker as a rum man. He was a wine gentleman, as far as they knew. At all of the neighborhood get-togethers he hosted, you could always find him offering (and drinking) the finest chardonnay on the street. The rum was reserved for nights like this one. Nights when he was alone, thinking and stewing.

He was leaving soon to go play neighborhood watchman for the night and wanted to self-medicate before walking out the door. Crocker felt on edge more than usual lately, and the drinking helped. His anxiety medication no longer seemed to work like it once used to.

He sat in his study, a large room punctuated with a grand, dark cherry-colored desk and lines of books in the wall's built-in bookcase behind it. He loved to read about almost everything. He'd get himself lost in books about war, guides for planting in your garden, and those cryptic blank-covered texts he referred to as those "other" books; the ones that felt dangerous when he held them. Those ones were hard to come by and they were always worth the effort. Especially one in particular.

His love of books gave him the desire to write one of his own one time. It was going to be a breakthrough for him, the story of a lifetime that would help launch him out of his mundane job as a town records consultant down at the sleepy town hall. Problem was it never happened. He had started it but then life got in the way, more specifically his wife's illness. All the time he had set aside to write his novel while outside of his day job ended up instead being spent caring for his wife. He didn't have the heart to finish it after losing her.

Crocker never let anyone else in his study. It was the one place where he could be himself, rum and all. Sitting at the desk, he poured himself another drink, this time straight with no filler. He threw it back, felt the burn hit the back of his throat, and started singing a Johnny Cash song out loud, the one about falling into a burning ring of fire where you go down and the flames go higher.

He stopped. That line always got him. *The Man in Black sure knew how to hit the hammer on the head*, Crocker thought to himself. Who knew how a song could so closely relate to your life? Written by a complete stranger, yet it feels like they took the words right out of your mouth as if they could read your mind. Crocker, with three glasses of rum running through his body, considered this.

"Well, that makes you one fine songwriting son of a bitch," he said out loud with a hearty laugh to the empty room. "Yessir."

He got up from his seat, a wobble in his step. "Speaking of which," he said.

Crocker fumbled his way around his desk and walked over to a wooden bin on the floor filled with all of Deborah's old vinyl records. They were his connection to her, and listening to them made him feel like she was still there in the room with him, arms draped over his shoulders and dancing with him the way she always used to, face-to-face and heart-to-heart.

"You've got no rhythm, Mr. Crocker," she'd often tease him.

"But I've got *you*," he said out loud now to the empty room, thinking of her. "You're all I've got ..."

A single tear fell from Crocker's eye as he flipped through Deborah's records. All the greats were here: The King, Roy Orbison, Bob Dylan, Tom Petty, Bruce Springsteen, and, yes, Johnny Cash. The record covers were old, many of them faded and discolored, but he knew the cover he wanted as soon as he saw it.

He gently slipped the black platter out of its sleeve and walked it over to a record player on a nearby table, holding it like a hungry person being careful not to spill a hot bowl of sacred soup. He put the record on the mat, lifted the player's needle and dropped it down onto the groove he knew by heart.

The sound of familiar horns filled the room, followed by that deep, foreboding voice that warned of love and wild desire.

THIRTY-FOUR

Artie's breathing had become worse that evening. Shallow, short breaths were all he could manage. When he didn't get up from the bed when Tommy called him for dinner, Tommy knew he had taken a turn for the worse.

"When was the last time he ate?" Tommy's mother asked him as they sat at the table. They were having precooked rotisserie chicken for dinner, something quick before Beth had to leave for her night shift at the nursing home. She worked around the clock to provide for her son and herself, keeping up on the bills and keeping their small home safe. Tommy's father was one of those guys who went out for a dump run and never came back. He left when Tommy was five, and if it wasn't for some photos Tommy found of him in a shoebox in the hall closet, Tommy wouldn't recognize his father if he saw him on the street. No need for that loser anyway, Beth was doing all right for herself and had found a renewed sense of happiness in recent years, although Tommy couldn't quite tell why.

Tommy looked over at Artie's food bowl where he had just placed a mix of special prescription wet food for kidney support next to regular wet food from earlier in the day that had sat there

uneaten and turned dry. Some bits of chicken he added on top to
entice Artie to eat didn't even work.

"He only nibbled at some of it this afternoon," Tommy said
to his mother.

The same could be said for Tommy, who was just picking at
his plate. "I know this is hard on you, Tommy. I know how close
you two are," his mother said. "It's hard on me too. Artie has been
good to us. He's loved us and we've loved him. And just like you, I
don't want to see him suffer."

"I ..." Tommy began and stopped to hold back tears. "I don't
want to say goodbye to him. I don't know how."

Beth reached her hand out to her son's. "You'll know how in
your heart when the time comes."

Beth got up with her plate. "I have to get ready for work," she
said. "Be sure to finish your dinner."

Tommy nodded to her and took a bite, although he had no
real desire to. When his mother left the kitchen, Tommy went
over to the cupboard and took out a jar of peanut butter. He
brought a spoon full of the peanut butter—Artie's favorite—into
his room and held it in front of the sick dog resting on the bed.

"Come on, Artie," he said. "Please, you need to eat
something."

Tommy moved the spoon closer to Artie's mouth and the dog
turned his head away from it. Tommy noticed that Artie wouldn't
even open his mouth, and that's when he remembered Dr. Finney
telling him that often times, near the end of life, animals and
people will show signs of lockjaw.

Tommy could feel tears coming and he tried to hold them
back again. He'd been trying to hold them back for weeks now
but it was no use. He dropped the spoon on the bed, wrapped his
arms around his friend, and cried. Artie placed his head on
Tommy's shoulder, returning his hug as best he could. Artie knew
what was happening, Tommy could feel it. When you have a
bond, a special connection with an animal like the one between

Artie and Tommy, you don't need words to know how each other feels.

"I'm not going to let it get you," Tommy said. "I'll do whatever I have to."

THIRTY-FIVE

J ack Balker sat on the deck in his backyard, under the non-stop flicker of the light that still wasn't fixed. After the disappearance of Milo, Jack found it hard to get himself to do much of anything, much to the chagrin of his wife. He spent most of his evenings just sitting on the deck, staring into the woods, waiting for some sort of sign. Waiting for Milo. Sam would periodically come out to see what his dad was doing, but he spent the majority of his time sad and alone up in his room reading comic books now, no longer enjoying the yard or summertime life with his dog.

And it was all Jack's fault, wasn't it?

"Stop being a child and sulking," Lindsey said to him on more than one occasion. But Lindsey didn't have to carry the weight of knowing her son's dog vanished under her watch. She never cared much for Milo, anyway. He was just an ornament to her, something to talk to her friends about who had their own dogs, a way for her to fit in with her new neighbors when they first moved to Sunfish Lane. Now that she was firmly cemented in with the local yahoos, she didn't need a dog to get on their good side or be in their inner circle to share recipes for casseroles that taste like dirt.

The sun was setting, creating a fire of oranges and yellows in the summer sky.

Another day down and another day of nothing, Jack thought to himself as he began to lurch up from his plastic chair. He took another bite out of the carrot-cake cupcake he brought home from work. He packed on a few pounds since the start of summer, eating his feelings, you could say. He stepped down off the deck with the half-eaten cupcake in his hand and walked up to the edge of his backyard, throwing the rest of the cupcake into the woods.

"For my homies," he said.

Jack turned back around, heading toward the house, when he heard a rustle not far from where he stood.

"Sam? Is that you?"

Another whisper of noise and quick movement came from the woods.

"Sam? You playing games, buddy? Come on, it's getting dark. Let's go in."

Jack heard the noise again, and this time there was something taking shape just on the other side of the trees. He looked up at the house and saw that the light in Sam's room was on.

Okay, not Sam, Jack thought, and started quickening his pace for the house. *If something is back there it will snatch me up the same way it did to Milo and no one will have a clue what happened to me.*

Lindsey was inside glued to the television, watching a reality show with a glass of wine in her hand, and Sam was upstairs probably wondering why his father was such a loser.

Jack's mouth became dry with fear, and he lost the sweet taste of the carrot-cake cupcake. His power walk for the house turned into a sprint. He was just about to reach the deck steps when he heard a jarring wail from behind him. Out of nowhere he felt an enormous weight come crashing down on his back, tumbling him down to the ground.

"Stop! Get off me!" Jack cried, swinging his hands with his

eyes closed. "Stop! I—" He felt a wet warmth go up and down his face. Jack opened his eyes.

"Jesus!"

Milo was on top of him, covered in dry blood and dirt.

"Milo?!" Jack said, not feeling the words come out of his mouth.

The dog gave him another lick on the face.

The back door opened up. "Dad are you okay? I heard—"

Milo barked at the sound of Sam's voice and Sam instantly started crying. He ran to his dog and embraced him.

"Milo!" Sam cried out.

"He's home, son. I can't believe it."

"But how?" Sam asked, tears in his eyes.

"I don't know," Jack said. "He looks like he's been through hell. Whatever's out there, he barely got away from it."

Jack gave Milo a good pat on the head, his heart feeling lighter than ever before. "Good boy," he said, ruffling Milo's clumped fur.

Jack got back up on his feet. "Come on, let's go clean him up."

"Yeah, Milo, you smell!" Sam said. Milo gave him a big lick on the face and Sam laughed.

The three of them began walking up the deck steps together, Milo a bit delicately, when Sam came to a stop.

"What's wrong, bud?" Jack asked.

"Dad, there's somebody who needs to know about this right away."

THIRTY-SIX

The kids at school would've had a field day if they saw Sweaty Sam Balker running down Sunfish Lane with his perspiration working overtime.

Sam had taken off out of his backyard so fast that Jack didn't have time to ask his son where he was going. Sam's stomach was filled with a knot of nerves and excitement as he approached Tommy's house. He couldn't wait to share the news with Tommy that Milo had returned, but he also felt it necessary that Tommy knew so that he wouldn't try going back in the woods on his own to search for the dog again. Sam didn't have any concrete reasoning to think that Tommy would do such a thing—Tommy didn't make any promises that he would—but in Sam's young mind the world revolved around him, and everyone was doing something either for or against him.

He got up to Tommy's driveway and saw that there was no car parked out front but plenty of lights on inside the house. He made his way up to the front door and knocked on it. No answer. He peeked into the window and saw a kitchen table set with a rotisserie chicken and one plate, but no one in sight. He knocked again, beginning to regret his decision to make the trek over and wishing he had waited until the next day. Or maybe he shouldn't be here at all? Maybe Tommy was just like all the other kids at school? Tommy came across like someone he could trust, someone he might even be able to consider a friend, but perhaps Tommy had had his fill of Sam already after that one trip into the woods together and was now a card-holding member of the Anti-Sam Fan Club, where the first step of initiation is to avoid Sam Balker.

"Tommy!" he yelled, hoping he wouldn't get in trouble for doing so, and hoping he was wrong about Tommy no longer wanting anything to do with him. Still no answer. Not even a response from Artie. "Just wanted to tell you Milo came home," Sam said, defeated.

Sam turned to leave when something caught his attention: Tommy's bike was nowhere to be seen. Tommy always kept his bike leaned up against the side of the house closest to the trash barrel. Sam knew this from driving by in the backseat of his parents' car and seeing it there all the time.

No bike and no Artie? Sam wondered. That could mean only one thing.

Thirty-Seven

Tommy rounded the corner of Sunfish Lane in a hurry, pedaling as fast as he could ahead of the rising moon. Artie sat in a ball in his milk crate attached to the front of the bike. Instead of holding his head up how he normally would, he stayed hunkered down.

Tommy kept glancing down at his friend to check on his breathing. The blanket Artie was wrapped in rose and lowered increasingly slower each time he inhaled and exhaled.

Time.

The one thing we never have enough of. That invisible commodity that is so sought after and wanted in desperate moments like this. Your mind will race as you try to think of all the different ways you can make up for lost time, time forgotten, time wasted. No matter how hard you try to ignore the feeling in the back of your mind, you always know it's a wasted effort, a shadow you can't outrun. You can't reverse time; you can't change it. It's in the moment you're living, just that one moment. All the others have passed, never to be repeated. And the ones still waiting? They may never happen at all.

Or they just might not be the ones you want to happen.

Tommy knew what he wanted. He knew what he needed, and not just for himself.

He squeezed the brakes, stopping his bike. Artie didn't move a muscle to see what was happening.

"Hold on," Tommy said.

Tommy reached in the milk crate and scooped up Artie. The bike fell to the side with a clumsy thud and Tommy couldn't have cared less. He had only one thing on his mind right now.

The blanket wrapped around the sick dog was becoming undone and Tommy had to bundle Artie back up. His face poked out from the blue blanket and the light from the moon illuminated it. That sweet face with the long whiskers and big, brown eyes seemed strangely calm to Tommy. There was a fleeting moment when Tommy let his self-doubt take over him like a discouraging blow to the gut.

It passed. It had to. He wouldn't let it freeze him in his tracks. He'd made too many mistakes before because of his second-guessing, his inability to be confident and pull the trigger when he needed to the most. But not now. It couldn't happen again. He wouldn't let it.

Tommy managed a smile for his dog.

"Hang on, Artie," he said. "We'll be home again soon."

He held Artie tight to his chest and gave him a kiss. The two of them disappeared together into the mouth of the woods.

THIRTY-EIGHT

I'm sorry he put you up to this," Jerry said, eyes fixated on the video game on the television screen. He was playing Zero-Man, a superhero character battling a two-headed goat and he was getting his butt whupped. Jerry threw the controller down in frustration.

"I'm serious, Jerry. You're not going to go check?" Sam asked.

Sam was standing in Jerry's room, something neither one of them ever expected to happen. In a moment of desperation and not knowing who else to turn to for help—someone who might actually believe him—Sam decided to try his chances with a person who he knew Tommy was friends with. Unfortunately, something seemed to have apparently come between the two, and Sam wasn't sure what.

"I've already been out there once before with him and I don't want to go back there again," Jerry said. "Like, ever."

"You have?"

"Yes, and I'm sorry but—"

"But you two are friends," Sam cut in. "Aren't friends supposed to stick together? Help each other out? He could be out there by himself running into that *thing* again."

Give the kid credit, Jerry thought to himself. Here was Sweaty

Sam Balker, the butt of countless lunchtime jokes and three grades lower than him, sounding like he wasn't going to back down. Jerry couldn't help but be impressed.

Jerry sighed, shutting his video game off and picking up his inhaler. Zero-Man would have to resume battle with the two-headed goat monster later.

"Okay, okay, you're right," he said. "I'll get the rest of the guys and we'll go check. If he has Artie with him then maybe something really is wrong. That game sucks anyway."

THIRTY-NINE

The clicker was working wonderfully tonight for Rooney as he clicked back and forth to his heart's content between the stations on his outdated television set. It turned out all he needed was a new pair of batteries to get the keys to his ship working again. Now he was back in his captain's seat, sailing the seas of infomercials, reality television, and the never-ending onslaught of apocalyptic news, all with his collection of fish swimming around him. The water was calm tonight and he was enjoying the view until he heard some commotion coming from somewhere outside of his ship on port side.

Rooney turned the volume down on the TV, silencing a Botoxed housewife mid-sentence. There it was again, some kind of faint chatter.

"Now what is it?" Rooney groaned. He pulled himself up from his seat with some extra effort and balanced himself once he was fully standing. The living room was dark, save for the glow from the television and the eerie blue hues the fish tanks emitted around the room and nearby kitchen; the faded green wallpaper in the living room looked like it was painted with a blue glow stick, as did the white tiles in the kitchen. Rooney had fallen asleep after supper and when he woke up, he never bothered to turn any lights on, except for the one coming from the television. His half-eaten meatloaf still sat on the table next to his chair.

Rooney shuffled over to the window facing the front yard, slowly pushing the faded curtains back just enough to take a peek outside without being noticed. Down at the bottom of the hill his house rested on, near his front yard but off to the side where the woods started, was a group of kids with bicycles having themselves a chat. A very serious one from the looks of it, Rooney thought.

"Little bastards," he muttered. Rooney took a closer look, squinting his old eyes and peering out of the window. He was trying to count how many of them there were when he noticed they were Tommy's friends, but there was no Tommy in sight.

"I swear if this kid went and muddled this all up," Rooney said as he made his way to the front door, picking up his cane along the way and throwing on an old beige jacket covered in stains. He couldn't afford to catch a chill, especially at his age.

Rooney opened the door with a loud creak that echoed through the silent night, catching the attention of Jerry, Eric, and Justin.

The three boys turned their heads at once.

Rooney, with their attention all his, called out: "What the hell do you think you're doing down there?"

Jerry gulped. "Holy crap. It's Old Man Rooney."

On the tip from Sam, Jerry had corralled Eric and Justin with no real great difficulty to see what was going on with Tommy. Sure, none of them wanted to go back into the woods, but they couldn't ignore the possibility of Tommy being out there on his own. Sam stayed behind at the suggestion of the three older boys.

"I said what's going on down there? And where's Tommy?" Rooney called out.

"Did he just say Tommy?" Justin asked.

"Sounded like it," Eric said. "Why would he ask us about Tommy?"

"You all deaf or what?" Rooney yelled, growing more and more impatient.

"We hear you!" Justin called back. Then, to his two friends: "We should go up there and see what he knows. Maybe he saw Tommy come through here."

Jerry balked at the idea. "Go up to Old Man Rooney? *Old Man Rooney*? Are you insane?"

"Come on, Jerry," Justin said. "You don't really believe those rumors about him, do you? We're running out of time here, anyway."

"I agree," Eric added. "I don't trust him for a second. Look, he doesn't even have any lights on in his house."

Justin let out a huff of annoyance. "You guys suck. Fine, I'll go talk to him by myself."

Justin started for Rooney's house. Jerry and Eric looked at each other and followed, two steps behind.

"How do you know our friend? Did you see him here tonight?" Justin asked Rooney as he made his way up the hill and stepped closer to the old man. "We can't find him."

"You can't find him?" Rooney repeated.

"Or his dog. They're both missing."

"Goddammit!" Rooney yelled, slamming his cane down. His anger wasn't directed at the kids, it was directed at himself. "I knew I couldn't trust him."

Justin, Jerry, and Eric took a step back, not expecting the old hermit on the hill to snap into such a red anger so quickly.

"What are you talking about?" Justin asked, honestly perplexed.

Rooney didn't answer. He began muttering to himself, looking down at the ground. How could he be so careless? How could he think for one second that he could tell the boy all he knew and expect him not to go and do some asinine thing? He was too young, too upset to think straight or entrust with that information, and Rooney was too old and too quick to give the burden to someone else. Pawning it off seemed like a good idea at the time, a golden—albeit selfish—opportunity to take the weight off his shoulders that had been there for decades. *Let someone else deal with it,* he had thought. Except that line of thinking doesn't always work out in your favor.

"There is ... there is something your friend is starting that he won't be able to finish on his own," Rooney said, beginning to feel a wrench of guilt.

"You mean he's in trouble?" Jerry asked, not quite believing he was talking to Old Man Rooney. Rooney didn't share the same regard talking to the nameless boy on his front lawn.

"Ah, yes. Something like that," Rooney said, still turning over in his head the sudden change of events and what was going to happen next. He longed to be back in his seat next to his half-eaten meatloaf, even though he no longer had an appetite.

"Well then we gotta go help him!" Eric blurted out.

"You know something you don't want to tell us, don't you? Something that has to do with what we found out there in the woods," Justin said to Rooney, looking him over suspiciously. Rooney's guilt was clear and there was no hiding it.

"He has something of mine that is very, very dangerous," Rooney said, feeling small and culpable. "You need to take it from him and get it back to me."

"Why don't you come with us and help?" Jerry asked, not believing the words coming out of his mouth. They just seemed to fall out without any real thought to push them. "If you know about that thing in the woods, then we're going to need all the help we can get."

"I can't. I can't leave. Haven't left here in ..." Rooney trailed off.

Jerry stepped close to Rooney, who was still standing in the frame of the opened door. The dream-like blue light inside the house was sneaking out behind the old man, making him look like someone who just stepped out from another dimension.

"Old Man Rooney," Jerry started, clearing his throat. Rooney shot his head up at him. "I-I mean Mr. Rooney, with all due respect, don't you get tired of people around here calling you a hermit? Don't you get bored staying inside your house all the time? I know I did. Now's as good a time as any to leave. We can't go back there alone. The last time we were down there we almost didn't make it back. If you know something, anything, we could use all the help we can get."

Rooney let out a sigh.

"I remember when I was growing up. I had a group of friends like you," he said, sounding rough at first, then softening his voice. "Always tooling around the neighborhood, getting ourselves into trouble and never learning any better. Those were some of the best days of my life."

Jerry, Eric and Justin stood quietly, not sure what to make of Rooney's response.

"That Tommy, he's going to have a lot to sort through. He's lucky to have friends like you."

"Does that mean you're going to come with us?" Jerry asked.

"No, kid. I couldn't even if I wanted to," Rooney said, gesturing to his cane.

"Forget it. Come on, let's get out of here," Justin said to his friends. "We have to find Tommy."

The three boys turned to walk away. As Jerry turned his back to Rooney, he said, "I guess it's true what they say about you. You're just a sad old man after all."

Rooney acted like this didn't sting him, but it did. Even coming from some snot-nosed kid, it did. No matter how old you are, you still have feelings and vulnerabilities underneath all of that wrinkle-riddled tough exterior.

Rooney watched the three boys walk back down toward the street.

They're going right into a slaughter, he thought to himself. A sickness filled him and he suddenly felt like an absolute piece of shit.

He looked down at his old hands, his old feet. What good were they if they didn't serve a meaningful purpose? What good was *he* if *he* didn't *have* a purpose? The life he had led since the crash, the literal one that took his wife and the one that his life slammed into head-on, had been a sham. A woe-is-me pity party with him being the star of his own sad movie. Was it ever going to stop? He hadn't had a peaceful night's sleep in decades, constantly haunted by visions in his sleep too absurd and heartbreaking to bring into the daylight.

How could he live through another tragedy?

Rooney squeezed his old mahogany cane tight, steadying himself.

He eyed the first step down. *Just one at a time.*

He lifted his right foot out of the quicksand of fear that he felt trying to pull him back inside to where he could hide. His foot landed on the step and he almost fell until he quickly drew his cane forward and caught himself, letting out a sigh of relief. His left foot followed more easily. He made the next step and, before he knew it, he was standing on the grass in his front yard. He looked around like a newborn baby fresh out of the womb.

The world didn't explode, the sky didn't fall. He was okay. He was the farthest he'd been from his place of solitude in years and he was *good*. In just that extra couple of feet everything around him felt different. The air he breathed in tasted different, tasted fuller, richer. There weren't any walls to box him in, no two-story coffin of his own design.

He took another step with his cane aiding him, then another. Suddenly he was walking down the hill of his front yard and, for the first time in a long time, he felt *alive*.

"Hey!" he called out as he made his way to the street.

The three boys didn't hear him. They were arguing with each other.

"Hey!" Rooney called out again, louder.

Justin turned around first, then Eric and Jerry. Their mouths collectively dropped when they saw Rooney coming down the hill right behind them, showing off his seesaw walk across the grass.

"I might be an old dog, but I still have a few tricks up my sleeve," he said. A smile crept up from behind Rooney's beard, but the kids hardly noticed.

FORTY

Tommy took in a deep breath and could feel the cool, crisp air filling his lungs as he approached the wishing well. He held Artie in his arms. In his hand was a worn and ravaged book. Its spine was peeling and its black cover torn.

Eerie silence surrounded the boy and his dog, except for a few tree frogs rattling their calls from places unseen. Tommy expected to hear unnatural sounds coming from inside the well, but it was void of any sign of life this time.

A chill of looming autumn ran down Tommy's back.

Old Man Rooney claimed he had a way to break the curse and stop the thing wreaking hell in their neighborhood. Tommy agreed to help, something he surprised himself by signing off on. Rooney's story—as far-fetched as it might have sounded—had Artie in the wishing-well-monstrosity's sights next, and Tommy wasn't just going to ignore that. Sick or not sick, Tommy swore to himself to protect Artie until the very end, because he knew that's what Artie would do for him. He had to see it through, and now, with Artie getting worse by the second, it had become even more urgent than he had previously anticipated.

But this wasn't how Rooney asked him to do it, or when. The old man had given the boy strict instructions to follow and to notify him when he was going to execute them. Tommy had no real intention of doing either. He had to do this his way, because his way was the only way he could save Artie.

Tommy opened the book. The old pages stuck together and needed to be peeled apart. He thumbed through the chapters, trying to find the right one.

There were pages covered in text that didn't look like anything he had ever seen before, and drawings of weird geometric lines and sketches of eyeless people he tried to ignore.

As Tommy searched through the book, behind him a tall and skinny silhouette appeared between the trees in the dark like a watchful scarecrow. It moved toward him.

"Why are you sweating so much? Are you nervous?" asked Rooney as he shuffled out of the shadows, leaning on his cane.

Tommy gasped and dropped the book, and Artie almost along with it.

"I see you brought your lucky pooch with you. Good idea keeping him close to you tonight, although I think we both know why you really brought him here."

Tommy was tongue tied. He was caught.

"Give me that damn book," Rooney said. He hobbled over to the book on the ground and snatched it up.

Rooney ran his weathered hands across the book's cover.

"This here was my sister's. It's full of all her rantings and ravings, spells and whatnot. There's one in here she began reading to put this thing away." He paused for a moment, gripping the book tightly. "She didn't get the chance to finish it. I thought it was going to be you, but I guess I was wrong. Did you even remember what chapter it was I told you to read?"

Tommy didn't have an answer. Seeing Rooney out here was the last thing he expected.

Rooney caught sight of the wishing well and began staring at it as if under a trance. "I never thought I'd be back out here. I never thought anyone else would know how to awaken this thing.

I should have done this myself a long time ago, but here we are. I'm finally going to put it to an end. No more wishes."

"Wait, please," Tommy said, trying to get the right words together to plead his case.

"No, no more waiting," Rooney answered. "This is it. We're sending this wishing well back to hell."

Tommy could feel Artie's breathing, barely a movement now. Artie felt so light in Tommy's hands it was as if he wasn't even holding him. It was like he was already gone.

"You mean it won't work again after this?"

Rooney's annoyance bubbled over. "Of course not! We're not just destroying the beast, we're destroying its home! That's the only way to completely break the curse and be done with it once and for all."

Tommy looked down at Artie. The dog wasn't just gazing back up at Tommy, he was looking through him.

"I can't do that," Tommy said to Rooney.

"What do you mean you can't? You don't get a say."

"There's one more wish that needs to be made tonight. I'll help you kill that thing, but we still need that wishing well first."

"Are you out of your goddamn mind?" Rooney roared, momentarily silencing the nearby tree frogs. He was dumb-founded. "I ask you to put the monster back in the box and you think I'm going to let you take it back out again?"

"He's dying," Tommy said, gesturing to Artie. "It will be different when I do it. No one has to get hurt. This is the only way I can save him."

Old Man Rooney's eyes became cold gems in the dark, staring straight at Tommy from under his bushy eyebrows.

"You don't understand what we're dealing with," he said. "You think it will be different if you use it because you want it for a good cause. That's the same thing everyone thinks when they come here. That's the same thing my sister thought. Everyone who falls into this trap tumbles into it because of what they think in their hearts is a good reason. Every wish cast here has come from a place of good intention, but it always ends up a nightmare."

"I have to try," Tommy said, standing his ground and not letting Rooney shake him.

"No, you won't," Rooney snapped back. "Go home and be with your dog while you can. I'll do this myself."

Rooney, with a mix of frustration and focus on his face, reached into his pocket and pulled out a book of matches. "I'm lighting it up and ending it."

He began his march to the stone structure, book and matches firmly in one hand with his cane in the other. He bumped Tommy's shoulder as he walked past him.

"Go home," he repeated to the boy.

Tommy backed off, making his way out of the clearing and into the woods. He had no real intention of leaving, that wasn't an option. But he didn't know what to do next to prevent Rooney from going forward with destroying the wishing well before he could make his wish for Artie. All he wanted was to wish for Artie to be healthy again.

Tommy began panicking, asking himself *what should I do?*

Artie was running out of time and Rooney was in their way.

Rooney made it to the edge of the wishing well. He carefully opened the book to a specific page.

He cleared his throat and began to read: "Come, dear gods, from every realm, and give me your strength. Let me be your sword to strike this wicked beast down. For it is born out of fear, it is born out of death, and it does not belong. Let it be gone. With this prayer, let your powers be my action. Come, dear gods. Stir the creature awake!"

Rooney froze, waiting for something to happen.

Nothing.

Tommy, now in the dark of the woods, turned around and started for Rooney but stopped, not sure exactly what he was going to do. He wasn't going to knock an old man over, was he? No, he wouldn't hurt the old timer. But he would certainly take that book from him if it meant saving Artie.

"I said come now, stir it awake! For it must see the man who befalls it!" Rooney yelled abruptly. He looked over the edge and into the well, peering past the tangled mess of vines and into the darkness.

Not a sound.

"You in there, you son of a bitch? I need you to look at me before I can light your ass on fire."

"Oh, we see you clear as day."

Old Man Rooney turned around and dropped his book. What he saw nearly stopped his heart. It blocked out the moon in the night sky as it towered over him, white steam rising up from its crooked shoulders. But it wasn't its size or the rotting earth caked over the beast that made Rooney's skin crawl like the bugs feeding off of it; it was its face.

"We see him very well, don't we, my dear?"

From behind the behemoth stepped Carl Crocker, dressed in his everyday clothes in a very not-everyday situation. "Well, don't be rude, Rooney. Say hi! You must certainly remember my wife Deborah?"

"What have you done?" Rooney managed to creak out. He was stuck in shock. "What on God's green Earth have you done?"

The creature that stood before the old man was far worse than anything he had imagined or expected. Where the head of the body should have been there was a lopsided lump sticking up lackadaisically. In the center of it was what appeared to be half of a woman's face; it had only one hazy eyeball and its skin sagged terribly in a crooked angle. It looked miserable, like a caged animal that wanted to be let out.

Rooney saw a slug slink across its face and disappear up its nose.

"Let's be honest, God has nothing to do with this," Crocker said with a sinister smile. "Love comes in all shapes and sizes and this right here is absolute love. You of all people, Rooney, should know that the man upstairs has none to give, so we find it ourselves."

Tommy and Artie looked on, still in the woods surrounding the clearing. "Good thing we stayed put," he whispered to Artie.

Starting to shake, Artie let out a small whimper. Tommy thought for a second that Crocker heard him, but Sunfish Lane's watchman was too caught up showing off to Rooney to notice them.

Crocker started laughing.

"Or, I guess you could say we take a walk in the woods and make a wish," he said to Rooney. He twirled his hand around and tilted his head back and forth in an animated sing-song fashion. "If you wish upon a star, oh you can go so far!" he started singing.

"She's suffering, you bastard," Rooney said. He felt more rage now than fear.

"You don't think she looks good?! She looks more beautiful than ever. She's got that little twinkle back in her ... eye."

Crocker wrapped his arms around his wife's torso—as much as they would reach around the wide frame—and gave her a kiss on the arm. He couldn't reach her head. His mouth came back covered in that bizarre, orange ooze. Crocker wiped it away with his arm.

"Of course, she isn't very fond of being kept down there in that hole, are you honey?" Crocker said. "We had a couple little incidents of her getting a wee bit overzealous and taking off on her own without me. But I tracked her down, eventually. I think she did everyone a favor when she shut up that annoying Mrs. Skittles, don't you? And how about the head in the mailbox?! My girl still has a sense of humor!"

Crocker paused for a moment. "Well, I might've had a hand in that."

"I'm sorry about what happened to your wife, Crocker," Rooney said. "This ... this isn't going to bring her back. You know that."

Crocker's eyes darted back at Rooney. "Bring her back? For

shame, old man! You sound jealous. Having regrets about not using the well for your wife? You know there's always time. It's such a shame what happened to her in that crash. Luckily you made it out alive though."

Crocker's patronizing tone was not lost on Rooney.

"Don't you dare bring Helen into this," Rooney said, feeling his long, unkempt nails dig into his palms as he clenched his fists.

"You make this place sound bad," Crocker countered. "Your sister Janice certainly didn't think it was, did she?"

"Wipe that shit-eating grin off your face, Crocker. You and I both know that she lost control, the same way you are now."

"Oh boo-hoo, you're no fun," Crocker said. "I for one had my doubts about it at first, too. I remember growing up and hearing stories about what happened. When I was a kid, I could never find the place no matter how hard I looked. Eventually I just wrote it off as a small-town urban legend. But who knows, maybe I was lacking faith. Or a reason. It's funny how you can find an oasis in the desert if you're thirsty enough. Stopping by at Sherwinkle's bookshop and paying him a little extra to come up with the right literature to make this place work its magic didn't hurt, either."

Crocker reached out and held the deformed hand that now belonged to his monstrosity of a wife. "Heck, this place works miracles. Just look at us now."

Rooney ripped a match out of the matchbook, mumbling something to himself.

Crocker let go of his wife's hand and cautiously stepped toward Rooney. "Now, old man, don't go and do something stupid. We really have a busy night ahead of us. I promise once we're done here you can have your turn and wish Helen back. Hey, we can have a double date!"

"I told you once already: Don't. Say. Her. Name."

Rooney quickly struck the match, creating a flicker of yellow light in the dead, pale glow of the moon-lit woods.

Crocker sprang from his soft steps into a leap, tackling the old man down to the ground. Rooney dropped the matchbook along with the lit match, lighting some scattered brush on fire. It quickly spread, encircling the wishing well with dancing flames.

"Now look what you've done, you fool!" Crocker yelled as he pinned Rooney down by the throat with his own cane. Spit came out of Crocker's mouth like a rabid animal. This was certainly not the Carl Crocker that Judy Simmons was dreaming about when she cooked that meatloaf.

Rooney was choking, trying to push the cane off himself and alleviate the pressure, but he wasn't strong enough to lift it against the much younger and stronger Carl Crocker.

Tommy, seeing this, turned to Artie in his arms. "I'm going to have to go in there. I can't leave him. I'll be back as soon as I can."

He gently placed the dog, still wrapped in his blanket, down on a soft area of grass. Even though Artie was becoming increasingly lethargic, Tommy knew his dog was well aware they were in danger. The reflection of the fire in Artie's eyes told Tommy that as sick as he was, he wasn't gone yet.

"You wait right here, okay?"

Artie shifted his gaze from the struggle at the well back to Tommy, giving him that knowing look.

FORTY-ONE

A wooden cane that he entrusted to help get him around everywhere was now ironically the thing that was keeping him down, Rooney thought to himself. *Well, that and this asshole who won't get off me.*

"This is your own damn fault," Crocker said, still pushing the cane down on Rooney's throat. "If you just minded your own business you could be at home right now eating English muffins or doing whatever it is you old geezers do."

"I ... prefer ... bagels," Rooney croaked out.

Crocker started laughing, spit spraying out of his mouth. He felt pure joy choking the life out of this old man until it was quickly replaced with confusion and a sharp blow to his side. He tumbled from off of Rooney and onto the ground beside him, experiencing a sickening sense of déjà vu.

Crocker looked up and saw Tommy on top of him, holding him down with a knee lodged in his stomach and his arms locked to the ground.

"I should've known it was you," Tommy said.

"Kid, why don't you go run home to mommy and maybe I'll forget I saw you here."

"Problem with that," Tommy said, pressing his knee in harder, "I won't forget I saw you here."

Crocker let out a groan of pain. He tried pushing Tommy's hands off his arms and couldn't; there was a rock directly under the center of his back, giving Tommy plenty of leverage as it dug deeper into Crocker's spine each time he tried to get back up.

"Deborah!" Crocker blurted out, pissed as ever that a kid had the upper hand on him.

The hulking deformity Crocker now considered his wife had been standing idle, watching and waiting for its love to ask for its help. With the call of its name, it blinked its one sad eye in recognition and bellowed a guttural call back.

"You want to eat tonight?" Crocker yelled. "Then get over here!"

The pitiful look on the half-human face of the beast snapped into a savage snarl. Short, sharp teeth, that were more brown and black than white, curled from its grotesque mouth. It reared itself back and charged at Tommy with heavy, thunderous steps. A blinding red light shined out from its open mouth as it grew bigger and bigger, much larger than any mouth should be.

Ding! Ding!

The beast came to a stop and waved its mangled arms in the air like it was trying to swat away a fly, slashing its long, sharp fingers—the same ones that caused prickles of fiery pain for poor Sam Balker—in useless defense.

Ding! Ding! Ding!

Crocker's nightmarish wife let out a frustrated cry of pain and grabbed its head. It leaned over to try and shield itself.

"Nice shot!"

"Told you I could hit the head!"

"Do it again!"

Ding!

The beast grabbed its head again and fell to one knee.

Ding! Ding!

The oh-so-familiar sound to Tommy grew louder and louder. He turned and saw his three pals, Jerry, Eric, and Justin, come running out of the woods with their aluminum baseball bats in hand. They each had a plastic bag full of rocks from Jerry's driveway wrapped around his shoulder and were pelting Crocker's wife with them.

Tommy felt a sensation of pride well up inside of him. And something else: hope.

"How'd you guys know I was here?" he asked his friends while still keeping Crocker pinned to the ground.

"Sam Balker said you were in trouble," Justin said. "When we found out you weren't home, we figured there was only one place you could be at this time of night."

The three kids circled the beast, hitting it again and again, one after the other. It tried to get up and each time it did one of the kids would nail it in the face, sending it back to its knees.

"Jeez, Mr. Crocker," Jerry said, taking another rock out of his bag. He had a new bat in his hands after leaving his other one behind the last time he was at the well. "I think your wife might need a face lift."

"I should've let you die you little shit," Crocker spat out from on his back.

"Okay, Tommy. We got it down," Eric said. "Now how do we finish it?"

Tommy and Crocker both looked at each other at the same time and then over at the nearby book of matches on the ground next to Rooney. The old man had his hands around his throat and was still trying to catch his breath.

Tommy pushed off of Crocker to lunge for the matches, thinking that if he could kill Crocker's abomination while outside of the wishing well—and without destroying the well itself— there would still be a chance to make his wish for Artie, in spite of Rooney's warning.

The book of matches was a few feet away from Tommy's grasp. He vaulted toward it, landing a few inches short. The heat of the fire encircling the wishing well cast a blanket of warmth over his face as he crawled closer to the matchbook. The fire was within arm's reach and Tommy had to squint because the growing flames were so bright. He had his back turned to Crocker and was about to pick up the matches when he felt a sudden bite of extraordinary pain in his right ankle, followed by another that shot up his leg.

Tommy screamed. He looked down and saw the tip of his right foot facing the wrong way. Crocker had a hand wrapped around it and was trying to drag Tommy away from the matches. In his other hand, Crocker had his police baton up in the air and was about to bring it down for another strike.

In shock, and in more physical pain than he had ever experienced before, Tommy kicked back with his free foot, hitting Crocker point-blank in the face. He felt something give and when he pulled his left foot back, he noticed Crocker's front teeth were no longer in his mouth.

"Goddammit!" Crocker yelled, falling back and putting his hands to his mouth, dropping the baton to the ground. Dizzy with pain, he landed on the dirt next to the baton, and head first into the fire.

Crocker let out a wail of agony so morbid it made the screams people made in all the scary movies Tommy had ever seen seem childish.

Crocker frantically rolled away from the fire, covering his entire face, his hands trembling. He let out muffled shrieks like a madman. Tommy could hear a hot sizzling sound as Crocker's flesh burned.

Tommy coiled back, writhing in his own world of pain and putting his hand to his ankle. He felt like he was going to simultaneously throw up and pass out until he heard his friends calling for help.

"Hurry, Tommy! This thing is getting back up and we're running out of rocks!" Eric said from behind.

Tommy blocked out the pain as best he could and hopped forward on his one good foot, snagging the matchbook and making his way to his friends. He took out a match and struck it. He held the small flame in his hand and aimed it at the monster in front of them.

"This is it," he said. "You're going to hell where you belong and I'm going to save—"

The flame blew out, and so did the air right out of Tommy. He crumpled to the ground, holding his crotch and gasping to catch his breath. From on his knees facing the ground, Tommy could see in the corner of his eye two brown dress shoes step out from behind him.

"You dumb kid," he heard Crocker grunt slowly and deliberately in an unrecognizable husky voice, getting as much as he could out of each syllable. "This isn't a movie. You don't get some fairy-tale ending."

Tommy looked up at Crocker's face. It was a wretched mix of melted flesh and dirt. One of his eyes had gone black and strings of skin hung from him like spaghetti, revealing bone. His perfectly brushed hair was gone, replaced with a charred dome that emitted a light smoke. His nose, now brittle and small, left a hole in the center of his face. There was a crimson flow of blood pouring down from his now-lipless mouth and all over his black department-store polo shirt. The khaki shorts he was wearing likely didn't stand a chance, either.

"And that goes for all of you, too!" he yelled at Tommy's friends, sneering in ghoulish delight. "This is *my* neighborhood! You shouldn't have come back here! You little pissants are about to get stepped on."

Crocker laughed hysterically. He turned his attention back to his wife. "Honey, I'm home!"

The behemoth the kids surrounded surged back to its ragged and stumped feet. Jerry, Eric, and Justin desperately hit it with the remaining rocks as fast as they could but they were no longer having any effect; the beast was feeding off of Crocker's love. Jerry took the bag off from around his shoulder and began madly clubbing the beast with his bat. The others followed his lead. Crocker's wife just stood and took the punishment as if it didn't care. Each swing was met with an audible wet crack as orange ooze leaked from its mushy body. The ooze stuck on their bats and slowed their swings as if they were caught in a giant spider web.

"Oh, we have flies in our web tonight, darling," Crocker said with a toothless grin. "Shall we begin?"

The creature in the center of the action made a sound that was half jubilation and half prehistoric.

Yuc! Yuc! Eeeeeee!

Crocker's creation reached out and pulled Eric's bat out of his hands. It swiped its jagged claws at him, cutting Eric across his face and momentarily blinding him. He screamed, covering his face with his hands. Blood seeped out between his fingers. Justin tried hitting it again from behind, but the beast turned around and rushed into him like a linebacker. Justin flew back, feet off the ground, and hit a tree. He tried to get back up and collapsed.

"Stop this, Crocker!" Tommy yelled.

"Tommy," Jerry said, with his bat at the ready and fear in his eyes. He took his inhaler out of his pocket and inhaled a puff. "We tried. I'm sorry."

Jerry got in his hitter's stance as if he was standing at home plate in the bottom of the ninth with the winning run in scoring position. Crocker pointed at Jerry, and Tommy heard a grunt of acknowledgment from his wife before it began running at the batter.

The beast crunched its head down like a bull in a bullfight. Jerry pulled his bat back, a locked and loaded slingshot ready to fire. Crocker's wife was right in front of him in a flash. Jerry swung as fast as he could, making direct contact with the awkward space where the creature's uneven head melded on top of its crooked shoulders.

The aluminum bat broke, cracking into two pieces right down the middle.

Jerry froze. The beast shot its head up and grabbed Jerry by his hair. It slowly lifted him up off the ground, dangling him.

Jerry kicked and yelled, swiping at the beast's large hands to break free, but he couldn't reach them. For a moment, Tommy thought he heard the monstrosity chuckle. Then it tossed Jerry into Justin like a piece of crumpled up paper into a trash bin.

Crocker clapped, an unhinged ringmaster at the center of his own evil circus enjoying the evening's show.

"Well done, my love."

He smiled at Tommy, who was bent over helplessly on the ground in pain and clutching his twisted ankle. It was clearly broken and Tommy was starting to go into real shock. The good thing about that was at least the pain was beginning to become somewhat numb.

"Officer, it was terrible. These boys beat up that old man and then got into a fight with each other over who was going to take his wallet. I tried stopping them but they kept swinging their baseball bats at me. I had no choice. I had to defend myself," Crocker recited with a disturbing display of fake remorse. "Maybe I'll say something along those lines," he said, walking in stride toward Tommy. "I mean, after all, who are they going to believe, me or a bunch of brats?"

He laughed with a hearty bellow, placing his hands on his stomach.

Seeing Crocker this way now helped Tommy realize two things: First, he was right not to trust the "neighborhood savior," and second, he would never allow himself to back down from a bully.

"Shut up," Tommy shot back at him. "You actually think you're going to talk your way out of this? That slimy charm of yours—that act of yours—can only last for so long. Sooner or later it's going to catch up to you and you're going to have nothing left. No home, no friends, no psycho-bitch monster to make you feel better."

Crocker squatted down. His remaining, piercing eye held tight on Tommy.

"Ah, and then there was one," he said, with what was left of that patented Crocker smile glowing through the dark, encrusted blood on his face. "You know, Tom, your mom is awfully pretty. We don't want anything to happen to her that will change that, do we?"

A flash of anger burned through Tommy and he tried getting up, leaping at Crocker, before falling back down in the dirt.

Crocker laughed again. "Touched a nerve there, I see. Bit of a momma's boy?" Crocker dropped the smile.

"Everyone's got someone except for me. I've had everything taken from me and now that I've finally found a way to get Deborah back, you expect me to let you take that, too? Who are you to decide? You're just some kid who's going to amount to nothing. I had a life and I'm getting it back, no matter what."

Crocker's abomination of a bride took its place at his side.

"No more games. It's time for you to become complete for me," he said to it. "You're past the furry appetizers. Now it's time for the main course."

Deborah looked at Crocker with scared apprehension, seeking approval.

"Eat," he said simply.

The beast homed in on Tommy. Its apprehension was gone, replaced with the heavy panting of bloodthirst, a beast in every sense of the word. Its wet, foul-smelling mouth opened, revealing a rotting tongue missing quarter-sized portions of flesh. Its brownish-black jigsaw teeth popped a bubble of saliva that was growing the more its mouth widened.

That mouth could easily fit both me and Artie, Tommy thought to himself as he looked into it.

The beast curdled with the relentless anger of a rattlesnake ready to attack. The red glow that had blinded Jack Balker and caused Milo to escape was starting to brighten from within the beast's mouth. Tommy put his arm up to shield his eyes from it.

"Eat and be merry," Crocker said, smirking at Tommy from behind the light.

The screeching war cry grew louder and louder. Tommy

looked around but there was no one to help. Jerry, Eric, and Justin were knocked out and he couldn't tell if Rooney was still breathing.

Except ...

Ruff! Ruff! Ruff!

Artie's bark.

Tommy never forgot it.

The abominable bitch stopped its pre-meal boasting, overtaken by the fierce call of a canine in rescue of his friend.

Tommy whipped his head around and there he saw him: Artie, his faithful companion, even at the end of his road, still not backing down.

"Artie!" he cried out.

The small beagle stormed out of the hiding spot Tommy had placed him in. He ran into the clearing where Tommy now lay on the ground at the mercy of Crocker and his creation.

Crocker was amused. "And what does he think he's doing?"

In that moment, Artie didn't look sick at all. He looked like his old self again; he looked full of life.

Artie bolted right at the three of them, then did a quick turn past them without slowing down.

Crocker followed him until he went by.

"Poor thing got scared and took off!" he said, laughing at Tommy. "Now, where were we?"

Eeek! Eeek! Deborah squealed out, matching the sound of a hunted pig. Its short arms flew around in a flurry, trying to reach something behind its shoulders. It spun around and that's when Tommy saw Artie, hanging off its back with his paws dug in and mouth tearing away at it.

Artie had run past them so he could get a head start for a jump big enough to latch onto the beast threatening to hurt his friend. He locked on the center of its back where its arms had no chance of reaching him.

The abomination spun in frantic circles.

"Damn mutt!" Crocker yelled. He reached under his shirt and pulled out a small gun, a 9mm pocket pistol.

Tommy swallowed the lingering pain from his crooked ankle and lunged forward, grabbing Crocker's leg to distract him.

"Get off me!" he shouted at Tommy, pointing the gun down at the child. "I swear kid, I'll shoot."

"Take your shot."

Ding!

Crocker's eyes rolled to the back of his head and he fell to the ground, revealing Jerry behind him, half a bat in hand.

"Nice shot, Jeer!" Tommy yelled.

Jerry gave an exhausted smile and passed out.

Artie was still hanging on the back of the beast, the two of them spinning in circles. The beast was desperate to get the dog off its back and Artie wasn't budging. The monster Crocker had created was strong, but not as strong as Artie's spirit. The buzzing of Artie's growl began to drown out the sound of the monster's fading cries of anger. It was starting to lose energy and slow down.

The monstrosity twirled around unevenly, closer and closer to the ring of fire and the wishing well inside of it, and farther away from where Tommy helplessly watched. Tommy saw this happening with a pit of growing concern.

"Artie, watch out!"

The beast's foot caught on Rooney's cane. It lost its balance, did a half spin through the fire burning around the wishing well, and ran into the side of the stone structure. It teetered for a moment between staying above ground and falling into the hole.

"Get off of it, Artie!" Tommy yelled. "Jump!"

Instead of letting go of the beast, Artie dug in deeper, as if sensing his job to protect Tommy was almost accomplished, save for one last effort.

That effort sent the beast over the stone wall and into the wishing well, and Artie along with it.

FORTY-TWO

Silence. Then, a loud *thud*.

The thud that came from inside the wishing well rivaled the volume of the thud Tommy's heart was making inside his head. He couldn't believe what he just saw. He immediately tried getting up to run to the wishing well. His ankle wouldn't let him. Instead, he had to crawl across the clearing, scraping his elbows and grabbing clumps of dirt to pull himself forward. With each painfully slow inch of progress he made, he felt that sickening sensation of being caught in one of those dreams where all you want to do is run but can't.

Tommy didn't want to think about the beast landing on Artie or Artie being trapped down there with it.

Artie had to be okay. He had to be.

Tommy made it to Rooney's cane. He used it to pick himself up and hobbled on his one good foot through the simmering flames blocking him from the wishing well. The spits of fire were about waist high on him and a few momentarily latched on his pants before going out. He didn't think twice about them.

He made it to the wishing well. He leaned on its rocky edge and peered over.

Nothing.

Just darkness.

"Artie!" he yelled into the void. "Come on, boy. Let me know you're okay." Tommy wanted to jump in there himself, shine a light on the damn place and—

Ruff!

"I hear you!" Tommy cried back. "I'm right here!"

But Artie wasn't the only one who responded. There was a short rustle, then a loud *BANG!* against the wall inside the wishing well. Rocks and dirt around Tommy became loose, cascading down below into the dark. Tommy had to hurry and he knew it.

"I can't see you, Art. Hold on"

Tommy took a branch off of the ground and stuck it in the fire behind him, lighting it and creating a makeshift torch. He pointed it down into the well.

At first, he didn't see anything, and then he saw him. Artie was hanging by his collar caught on a vine poking out from the rocks lining the inside of the well.

"There you are!"

Ruff! Ruff!

There was another loud bang from below, followed by a growl that certainly didn't belong to Artie. *No time to waste*, Tommy thought to himself.

How was he going to reach Artie? Artie was too far away to pick up, and if Tommy leaned too far over, he'd fall in and they both would be trapped inside. He raced through the options in his head, desperately trying to think of something.

Rooney's cane, he thought. *That's it.*

If he angled it right, he could loop Artie's collar around it and lift him up. But if he didn't get enough leverage, then Artie would slide off and—

"I won't let that happen," Tommy said out loud.

Tommy took Rooney's weathered walking stick, with its rough and angular crevices criss-crossing every which way, and stretched it down toward Artie while still holding the lit branch in his other hand.

Tommy was aiming the cane to hook Artie's collar when the beast banged against the wall again. For a split second Tommy felt the helpless motion of falling forward without having any way of stopping. He missed Artie's collar in the same fluid movement and instead got the cane stuck in the cracks between the rocks lining the other side of the wishing well. It propped Tommy up, stopping him from falling in with the beagle and the monster. He hung there for a moment. At first the cane felt as though it wouldn't budge and he thought he was stuck in limbo until it finally came loose. He pushed himself off and regained his upright balance, cane still in hand.

Close. Too close.

Tommy looked back down and noticed that Artie's collar was slipping off the vine more and more every time Crocker's creation slammed against the inside of the well. It wanted to get out and it didn't want to wait. Artie would be able to hang on for one, maybe two more impacts before he slipped all the way off the vine and fell to the bottom.

Tommy wiped his arm across his brow. "Okay, Art," he said. "I need you to stay very still. I'm going to put this cane through the opening of your collar and lift you up. Just hang on." Tommy gripped the cane tighter and leaned back in.

Artie was swinging back and forth from the impact of the beast's last hit. Tommy could see his white fur flash like a pendulum in and out of the light burning from the branch.

Below Artie, not far away, Tommy could also see the shape of the monster reaching up.

Tommy would have to time this just right to get the cane through the moving collar. If he waited for Artie to stop swinging, it might be too late.

He took a deep breath.

Artie was in the light.

Out of the light.

In the light.

Out.

Tommy darted the cane forward, making sure to do so in an upward scooping motion, and right away he felt the light weight of Artie on the other end.

"Gotcha!" Tommy said, pulling Artie off the vine.

As if on cue, the beast threw itself against the well's wall again, causing Artie to slip further toward the end of the cane and become heavier to lift. Despite the beagle's diminished weight, holding him up by one hand with what was basically a sturdy stick wasn't easy. Tommy could feel his grip slipping but hung on, scooping Artie all the way up and out of the wishing well.

Artie still had his eyes concentrated on the beast below as Tommy lifted him up and out into the air, above the tight confines of the stone structure. He gently lowered Artie down to the ground beside him and slipped the cane out from under his collar. Tommy tossed his makeshift torch to the side.

Artie was shaking and concentrating on the well, ready to lunge at the beast if he saw it again.

"It's okay, Art," Tommy said, wrapping his arms around his dog. "It's okay now."

Artie jumped, not realizing he was in the safe hug of his friend. He looked up at Tommy and gave him a big kiss.

Artie was safe from the monster, but his shaking wasn't stopping. What scared Tommy even more were the long periods between each time he could feel Artie take a breath.

Artie saved Tommy, but now Tommy realized he couldn't save Artie, no matter how hard he tried. That unforgiving truth was right in front of him, laughing in his face despite all his best efforts, and it broke his heart.

"This isn't over yet."

Tommy looked up. It was Rooney, on his knees and with the black book in his hands.

"Son, you need to throw that stick of fire down there and kill that thing once and for all," Rooney said.

Rooney was right, and as much as Tommy wanted to ignore it, he knew he couldn't.

The monstrosity was getting louder and louder, angrier and angrier by the second. If they just let it be, a lot more people were going to get hurt. They had to kill it, and with it trapped in the wishing well and Crocker knocked out, this was their chance.

But destroying the well also meant letting go of any chance of saving Artie.

Tommy closed his eyes, saw the copycat nightmare of Crocker's wife, then opened them and saw Artie.

What would the wishing well do to Artie? Would he still be himself or ... something else?

Tommy put his hand on Artie's head. The beagle struggled to find the strength to nudge up to it. Tommy wiped a tear from his eye, picked up the burning stick, and stepped as best he could to the edge of the wishing well with Artie under his other arm.

Old Man Rooney opened the black book and began reading: "We each have only one true self, one of you and one of me. We each have only a finite amount of time before we die. For your time has come, so let it be, let your weary soul be set free."

Tommy dropped the burning stick into the wishing well. Crocker's creation thrashed, screaming out in pain. The pit that was once black as pavement was now lit bright. Deborah rammed itself into the walls of the well, harder than before, and all of the rocks began tumbling down on it from above. A beam of red light from down in the well shot up into the night sky, one last threat of the beast's existence before it burned out with the fire under the falling rocks. The circular edifice slowly lost its shape with every fallen rock and, eventually, the monstrosity that encaged Deborah Crocker's soul and lived in the wishing well became silent and disappeared under the rubble. All that remained was a small dip in the ground covered by a solid pack of dirty rocks.

No sign of any wishes, neither those granted nor those forgotten.

Tommy turned his back to the wishing well. He wrapped his

arms around Artie as he leapt through the simmering fire and back to the other side of the clearing. Artie felt weak in Tommy's arms. He felt cold. His breathing was now nothing more than a faint up and down. Tommy sat down in the clearing, cradling Artie.

One by one, Eric, Justin, and Jerry stirred awake. They saw Tommy and Artie together and knew what was happening.

Justin picked up Artie's blanket and handed it to Tommy.

Tommy nodded thanks and wrapped it around Artie.

The three boys gathered around Tommy and his dog. Rooney respectfully kept his distance, having been through this before.

"There has to be something else I can do," Tommy said. "Something."

He felt a knot in his throat and started crying. A subdued feeling of embarrassment closed in on him. He was just a boy crying in front of his friends, after all. But it quickly faded away when one of them put a reassuring hand on his shoulder.

"Thank you, Artie," Justin said.

"Yeah, thanks, Art," Eric said. "You're the man."

Jerry kissed the palm of his hand and patted it on top of Artie's head.

"Coolest dog in town," he said. "I'd fight evil with you any day of the week."

Artie looked at each of them, the fifth member of a group of childhood friends forever linked together.

His brown eyes turned back to Tommy. Looking at his beloved dog, Tommy noticed that Artie's sweet face, although tired, had an etching of triumph to it. They were all safe and Artie knew it. He had done his job and could rest now.

"I'll catch back up to you again someday, Artie," Tommy said.

He gave his faithful friend a kiss.

A moment later, Artie was gone.

FORTY-THREE

H ere comes the heater!"
Jerry wound up and hurled the ball to Eric sitting
behind home plate. Justin swung at it, catching
nothing but air. The ball hit Eric's glove with a loud *smack!*

It was the following spring after that final night at the wishing
well, and Tommy and his friends were back at the ballfield with
the whole summer ahead of them.

And they had a new member on their team: Sam.

When the truth got out—or, at least, a variation of it—the
Balker boy's parents didn't hesitate to let their son venture out
with Tommy. The rest of Tommy's friends' parents no longer told
them to keep away from him, either. They had indeed become
heroes, thanks in part to George Farrison, who vouched for them
following what happened at the wishing well. It turned out that
Farrison, the retired yet ever-vigilant security guard, had been
keeping an eye on Crocker after the meeting he held at his house.
Farrison found Tommy and his friends in the chaos in the clearing
and gladly cuffed Crocker, bringing him to the police.

Problem was, how do you explain to the authorities what
happened in the woods, especially when you barely believe it
yourself?

Farrison didn't need to, Crocker did it for him—reserving himself a permanent bed at the Brighton Falls mental institution. The story that made it into the *Brighton Falls Gazette* (yes, the boys also made it on the front page, with a slightly different headline than Jerry envisioned) said that Crocker suffered from a personality disorder and had a schizophrenic breakdown following the death of his wife, resulting in sporadic violent acts. Tommy and his friends, the paper said, found out about Crocker and were able to stop him before he hurt anyone else.

That was great, Tommy thought, but he knew who the real hero was.

As for Old Man Rooney, his word didn't carry much weight anymore, so he didn't bother trying to explain to anyone what really happened in the woods. Those who needed to know already knew. Instead, he sauntered back up to his house on the hill and has slept like a baby every night since.

Some things are better left unsaid.

"Man, Jerry. That fastball of yours is picking up some steam," Justin said as he tried to get the kink out of his arm from his missed swing.

"You should try out for the team this year."

"You think?" Jerry asked, genuinely surprised.

"Yeah, if you can find time to stop hanging out with Sarah Lackey," Eric chimed in from behind the home plate.

Believe it or not, Jerry had graduated from looking at Sarah Lackey's belly button to being her boyfriend during the intervening school year. Having his face on the front page of the Gazette might have had something to do with that.

"Ha-ha, real funny," Jerry said. "Okay, who wants to be the next out? I'm just warming up."

"Come on, Tommy!" Sam said, clapping his gloved hand and free hand together from his position between first and second base.

"I'll give it a go," Tommy said. Justin passed him the bat and he walked up to the plate.

Tommy's ankle was better. It still wasn't completely healed, that would take at least another six months. Nevertheless, it was out of the cast and getting strong again. He could finally put weight on it after spending all winter cooped up on the couch drinking hot chocolate.

"All right, Mr. Ankle. Let's see what ya got," Jerry said.

Jerry threw the ball. Tommy swung and came up empty.

"Wow, Justin's not kidding," Tommy said. It was true, Jerry had found his niche on the field and it was on the mound.

Jerry smiled a mile-wide grin. He threw the ball to Eric and right by the swing of Tommy's bat a second time.

"Two strikes," Jerry said. "I think this will be the first time I've ever struck you out."

Tommy gave a little smile of his own, choked up on the bat, and got ready for the next pitch.

Jerry cartoonishly spat on the mound, looked over at first base, pretending there was a runner there, and reared the ball back before launching it at the plate.

Tommy swung, making solid contact.

Ding!

The ball rocketed up into the air, landing in the tall grass of the outfield.

"Well, who's going to get that?" Jerry asked, upset with himself for giving up the hit.

The five boys watched a small dog come prancing around the corner, wiggle its way through the fence, and head for the ball.

The dog sniffed the ball for a moment, inspecting its newfound toy before picking it up and running away with it.

In the golden haze of the setting sun, it looked just like Artie.

AUTHOR'S NOTE

I wrote *Artie's Bark* after having lost my own real-life version of Artie, a rambunctious and fun-loving beagle/hound dog named Oscar. It was my way of coping with a tremendous amount of guilt I felt after he was gone; not because I felt like I didn't do enough to help him when he became sick, but instead believing I put him through too much at the end—took him to the veterinarian one too many times to try and save him—when what I should have done was realize it was time to let go and not prolong a painful last chapter for him. He was too good of a dog—too good of a friend—to be in pain, as many of you probably feel about your own four-legged partners who have fallen ill and ventured off into the unknown without us.

I don't think that guilt will ever totally go away. Writing *Artie's Bark* helped, but it's still there and always will be, I suspect. My hope is that *Artie's Bark* will help someone who reads it and is going through a similar situation or has already come out the other end and finds themselves in the same position I was left in after. I've heard that your amount of grief is equal to your amount of love for those you lose. There's no shame in talking about it, whether it's a person or an animal.

While my name is on the cover, there are a lot of other people who deserve recognition that I would like to thank, starting with my mom, Elizabeth Kelley, who would always say to me, "Why don't you write a book?" Well, here it is, although it might not be the kind you expected. To my grandmother, Beatrice Savio, who is an avid reader herself and has been looking forward to this, thanks for your continued enthusiasm and optimism—and sorry about the language. A big thanks as well to Nicholas Santos and Patrick Cassidy for reading early drafts of *Artie's Bark* and giving me the encouragement I needed to complete it. The same can be said for Tim Miller and Jon Tromp, who have always given me a boost of confidence and taken the time to read my work. Sending thanks to my father, Joe Savio, for his support and my uncle, Chris Kelley, who is partly to blame (and thank) for my fascination with all things spooky. Rachael, thanks for listening.

And last but not least, thank you to the folks at WordFire Press for giving me this opportunity to share my story with you.

—January 30, 2022

About the Author

Jason Savio was born and grew up in the town of Falmouth on a big sandbar known as Cape Cod. He has his master's in journalism from Emerson College in Boston and has written numerous stories for the *Cape Cod Times* and *Pulse Magazine*, interviewing familiar names  like Chevy Chase, George Thorogood, and Max Weinberg of Bruce Springsteen's E Street Band, as well as horror icons Kane Hodder of *Friday the 13th* and Doug Bradley of *Hellraiser* fame. He has been the proud dog dad of two loyal four-legged companions and has played the role of Master Splinter to a turtle for the past 25 years and counting. *Artie's Bark* is Jason's first novel.

Visit Jason online at jasonsavio.weebly.com and follow him at @artiesbark and @jasonrsavio on Twitter, and @jasonrobertsavio on Instagram and Facebook to get updates on *Artie's Bark* and see what he's working on next.

OTHER WORDFIRE PRESS TITLES

Selected Stories: Horror and Dark Fantasy
by Kevin J. Anderson

Season of the Wolf
by Jeff Marriotte

The Wolf Leader
by Alexandre Dumas

Our list of other WordFire Press authors and titles is always growing. To find out more and to shop our selection of titles, visit us at:
wordfirepress.com

facebook.com/WordfireIncWordfirePress

twitter.com/WordFirePress

instagram.com/WordFirePress

bookbub.com/profile/4109784512